Emory B. Lease

A Syntatic, Stylistic and Metrical Study of Prudentius

Emory B. Lease

A Syntatic, Stylistic and Metrical Study of Prudentius

ISBN/EAN: 9783337313029

Printed in Europe, USA, Canada, Australia, Japan

Cover: Foto ©Andreas Hilbeck / pixelio.de

More available books at **www.hansebooks.com**

A Syntactic, Stylistic and Metrical Study

OF

PRUDENTIUS

A THESIS PRESENTED TO THE BOARD OF UNIVERSITY STUDIES OF
THE JOHNS HOPKINS UNIVERSITY FOR THE DEGREE
OF DOCTOR OF PHILOSOPHY

BY

EMORY BAIR LEASE

Formerly Fellow of the Johns Hopkins University

BALTIMORE
THE FRIEDENWALD COMPANY
1895

Nobilissimus Hispanorum scholasticus.—*Beda, Gr. Lat. VII*, 256.

Nam similis scientiae viri, hinc Augustinus, hinc Varro, hinc Horatius, hinc Prudentius lectitabantur.—*Sidonius Ap. Ep.* 2. 9, 4.

Christianorum Maro et Flaccus.—*Bentley, ad Hor. C.* 2, 2, 15.

CONTENTS.

f. Participles, Gerund, etc.

g. Prepositions.

INTRODUCTION.

Prudentius, Rome's great Christian poet, flourished during the closing years of the fourth century and the early years of the fifth. He lived in an age luminous by the presence of such eminent Christian writers as Ambrose, St. Jerome, and Augustine, the Augustan age of Patristic literature; an age possessing the distinction of having produced Symmachus and Ammianus, "the last respectable representatives of the Roman religion in literature," the former, Prudentius' most formidable adversary; an age which produced Claudianus, and the great grammarians Servius and Donatus. Born in a distant province and spending the greater portion of his life remote from Rome, Prudentius soon became her best representative in the field that he had chosen. He was one of those children of Spain who gave to the Eternal City her best in more than one department of literature. Spain, the mother of Rome's greatest rhetorician, was also the mother of Rome's greatest Christian poet. Teuffel[1] pronounces Prudentius an "enthusiastic and artistic poet," and in referring to his verses in praise of the Christian faith and its martyrs, speaks of their "brilliant and picturesque style."[2] Others are no less loud in their praise. From the times of Sidonius Apollinaris down through the Middle Ages to our own time, he has been cited, quoted and praised.[3] "Prudentius," remarks Milman,[4] "even in Germany, was the great popular poet of the Middle Ages; no work but the Bible appears with so many glosses in High German, which shows that it was a book of popular instruction." Mico the Levite quotes more largely from him than from any other of the Christian poets.[5] But it was not in Germany alone that his works were read and admired. In other countries frequent references are

[1] Teuffel, Rom. Lit. (Transl. of 5th Ed.), §424.
[2] Idem, §436.
[3] Puech, Prudence, p. 36; Manitius, Christ. Lat. Poesie, p. 62; Sixt, Die lyrischen Gedichte d. Aur. Prud. Clem., pp. 1, 43; Ebert, Gesch. d. Lit. d. Mittelalters, I², p. 343.
[4] Milman, Lat. Christ., Bk. IV, Chap. 4.
[5] Cf. Ellis, Journ. Phil., 1893, p. 20.

made to him in the MSS. of various authors, and his poems are mentioned in the catalogues of a number of libraries.[1] His influence upon his successors, immediate as well as more remote, may be judged from the fact that he was imitated to a greater or less extent by Paulinus Petricordiae, by Sedulius, Alc. Avitus Ruricius, Fortunatus, Corippus, and Gregory of Tours.[2] He lived in an age when the classic poets were especially studied; when the Christian poets sought not only to rival them in strictness of technique, but also to revive the spirit of those models; when the literature proceeds from the schools and most of the authors are " rhetors " also.[3] It was largely an age of artificiality and false ornament, and Prudentius' writings show that he was not entirely free from these faults; some passages are obscure, some painfully prolix. He seems to have been not wholly unconscious of the dangers that his fatal copiousness exposed him to; cf. the close of the praef. to S. II: loquax lingua, 45; ventisque eloquii tumet, 58; fluctibus obruat, 65; sometimes he does not escape, sometimes he is submerged by the waves of his own verbosity. He wrote not as those mentioned by Lactantius,[4] nor as St. Augustine[5] himself, so much for the people as for the cultivated class of his time; and his wide acquaintance with the poets of Rome[6] as well as with the writings of the Church Fathers, the beauty and polish of many of his lines, his earnestness and fervor, must have won for him no small portion of the favor and esteem of that class. Nor further can it be maintained that his latinity is "confessedly impure," as has been done,[7] basing the statement upon the expression, "audi poetam rusticum," P. 2, 574. By this Prudentius does not wish to say that he wrote impure Latin, but, like Lucifer (p. 256, 7), that he felt that he was

[1] Manitius, SBer. Wiener Akad., 117 (1889) XII, 26; also Rhein. Mus. 1892, Suplb. p. 95.

[2] Manitius, in the SBer. (117); also Bonnet, Le Latin de Grégoire de Tours, Paris, 1890, p. 64: "Ses auteurs favoris parmi les chrétiens sont Sulpice Sévère, Prudence, Sidoine Apollinaire et Fortunat," Cf. also p. 50 f.

[3] Gröber, Grund. f. Rom. Phil., I, 379.

[4] Lact. V, 1, 9: Communi ac simplici sermone, ut at populum, sunt locuti.

[5] Augustine, Ps. 138, 20: melius est reprehendant nos grammatici quam non intelligant populi. (Referred to Hier. in Krebs Antil. I[6], 11.) Cf. also Ps. 36, 3, 6.

[6] Cf. §§ 145-148 : Prudentius as an Imitator.

[7] Ramsay, Dict. Biog. and Myth. (Prudentius).

no " rhetor," that his was only an unpracticed and inartistic style,[1] and the entire expression should be treated as a confession prompted by feelings of humility and of his own unworthiness. For his Latin in the main follows his models closely and is far superior to that of the other Christian poets. As Boissier says,[2] these public confessions are not to be interpreted too literally ; it was the fashion of the period to exaggerate one's shortcomings.

The object of the present work is twofold : first, a study of the syntactical and metrical usage of Prudentius, and, to a certain extent, of his style, together with a brief introduction on the Forms ; and secondly, a comparison of the latinity of that author with the latinity of Juvencus, an author of the same country and of the same century; to ascertain wherein they are alike and in what they differ, and to determine in this way the relation of Prudentius to his predecessor, aiming throughout to throw some light upon the latinity of the age. In order to facilitate such a comparison, the investigation has been pursued on parallel lines to those followed by Hatfield in his study of Juvencus, a plan based for the most part upon Draeger's "Syntax und Stil des Tacitus."[3] Comparisons are also made at different points with the usage of Vergil, more particularly in §§111, 112, 113, 118, 119, 141, 142, 143; and with the usage of Horace in §§145, 146. Parallel passages in other authors have also been added by way of illustration, chiefly through the assistance of the valuable indices of the volumes in the Vienna Corpus Script. Eccl. Lat.

The work is based entirely upon Dressel's edition,[1] which, though the result of a careful collation of some of the most important manuscripts and marking a decided advance in many respects over its predecessors, still has one conspicuous defect. Dressel has catalogued and described in the Prolegomena to his edition the manuscripts he used, but he was led into error in a number of cases from a lack of knowledge of the readings of the MS. Puteanus. This has been collated by Faguet,[4] p. 29 et seq. A number of minor errors, chiefly typographical, occur, among

---

[1] Sittl, Archiv f. d. lat. Lexicogr. 6, 560; cf. also Weyman, id. p. 294 : " Prudentius gehört keineswegs zur infima Latinitas."

[2] Boissier, La Fin du Pag., II, 106.

[3] Aurelii Prudentii Clementis Carmina, Dressel, Leipzig, 1860. A new edition of Prudentius by Joh. Huemer is promised in the Corpus Scriptorum Ecclesiasticorum Latinorum.

[4] Faguet, De Aurelii Prudentii Clementis Carminibus Lyricis, 1883.

4

which may be noted: silvae. for silvae, C. 8, 36; superatus for superatis, S. 1, 122; p. 225, foot-note to 181: Ov. Fast. II, 957 for 859; promitit for promittit, S. 2, 107; ccpit for cepit, S. 2, 350; sum for sucum, S. 2, 219. ande for ante, A. 218; Ps. 288. Index: aegis, 8 II for S II; sublime, S. V. 192 =?

4

ABBREVIATIONS.

A = Apotheosis.
C = Cathemerinon.
D = Dittochaeon.
H = Hamartigenia.
P = Peristephanon.

Ps = Psychomachia.
S1 = Contra Symmachum, I.
S2 =   "   "   II.
·pr attached = praefatio.
Juv = Juvencus (exc. in §152 c).

I.—FORMS.

§1. In Prudentius and other writers of the Fourth Century, the chief deviations from the classical forms are in the line of vulgarisms and archaisms. But to which of these categories a form is to be assigned is often a matter of very great difficulty.[1] Scholars are not always in agreement, take e. g. the form quïs (C. 3, 27) ; Wotke,[2] Sittl,[3] and Weise[4] regard it as an archaism, while Riemann[5] and Wölfflin[6] assign it to the sermo familiaris ; cf. also §19b. Both views may be right, as the vulgar and the archaic often are identical. In Prudentius there is less of the colloquial than in other writers of the same period, though the popular diction from the second century on was beginning to be used more and more freely even by the best writers, and to be found also in the official records.[7] Archaisms were introduced by the Christian poets as a matter of course ; Vergil had made use of them,[8] and he was their standard. So we find them often, one might almost say, zealously introduced.[9] A complete list of either the archaisms or of the vulgarisms would not be within the scope of this work. But some of the more striking and some used already by Juvencus will be given here, together with other peculiar forms. A list neither complete nor exact is given by Kantecki.[10] In **Declension** the following may be noted : *aquai*, A. 702 (used by Vergil, Aen. 7, 464 ; probably from him) ; such forms occur about 25 times in Plautus, cf. Trin. 359 (Bx), (Neue, I, 11, and

[1] Cf. Schulze, De Sym. Voc. Form., p. 115.
[2] Wotke, Wien. Stud. 1886, p. 130.
[3] Sittl, Jahresbericht, 1891, p. 232.
[4] Weise, Char. d. lat. Spr. 1891, p. 88.
[5] Riemann, Étude s. Tite-Live, p. 18.
[6] Wölfflin, Phil. 34, 137.
[7] Teuffel, R. L. §385, 3.
[8] The archaisms in Vergil, as noted by Servius, have been recently treated by Steele, Am. Journ. Phil. 1894, p. 164-94.
[9] Cf. also Symmachus, Ep. 3, 44 : "ἀρχαϊσμὸν scribendi non invitus adfecto"; also Sittl, Comment. Woelff. p. 408.
[10] Kantecki, De Prudenti Genere Decendi, 1874.

II⁹, 46 cites only 18 forms); in Vergil 4 times, Luc. Mueller, Re Metr.⁹ (1894), p. 472. *animabus*, S. 1, 531; P. 2, 289; occurs also in Auson App. 1, 36; Hier. Math. 4, 24, 19; Ep. 98, 1; in Priscillian,¹ frequent in Claud. Mam. 60, 10, etc.; also in Lat. transl. of the Book Sirach, 30, 7 and the Book of Wisdom, 14, 11. *pecua*, P. 10, 333; Apul. Met. 2, 1; Min. Fel. 36, 5, et al. *simplus*, P. 10, 878. The archaic *duelli* occurs Ps. 21 (also in Juv.), and *duello* Ps. 575; (*duellum*, Commod. 2, 10, 1). *olli*, ollis, (cf. Quint. 8, 3, 25) occurs: H. 139, 544, 730, A. 305, cf. Arnob. 197, 19; Cypr. Gall. Ex. 197; also Inscript. Hisp. No. 6278, 25. *hisce*, S. 2, 880; *hasce*, P. 10, 496. *discolora* (fem.), P. 10, 302. *prosapia*, C. 11, 89; Pspr. 36; P. 10, 112; 180; (an archaism; cf. Quint. 1, 6, 40) occurs 15 times in Lucifer Cal. and not infreq. in eccl. writers.⁹ *deitas*, A. 13, 1008; H. 96; Goelzer³ does not cite Prud. as using this word, and Wölfflin⁴ omits Prudentius from his list of those using this word, as also of those using prosapia. *induperator*, S. 1, 147; appeared in Enn. Ann. 5, 350; also in Alcuin and Theodulf.⁵ *stipis* (for stips) occurs in S. 2, 911, though MSS. Widmannianus and the ed. of Weitz read stipes. *quis*, for quibus, appears 12 times⁶ (12 also in Juv.); used by Plautus at least 4 times (Lorenz, Most. 1040, says only once; but add Curc. 552, Trin. 1038 and Amph. prol. 4.); frequent in Cypr. Gall. *isdem* occurs in C. 12, 86; S. 2, 603; 799; 805. *ossuum*, P. 2, 532; 5, 111; used before by Pacuvius and Accius, according to Priscian, Gram. Lat. 2, 254 and 750 (Keil); also by Tert. resur. 30, 31 and 32; Ennod. p. 274, 4, (H.); Cl. Mamert. p. 72, 9; 174, 24 (E); Vulgate, Ezech. 24, 5; Leges Burgundionum, 128, 12. *Vulgus* is twice used as masc., P. 6, 51, and S. 1, 580; so used in Juv. 4, 611; Riemann says this belongs to the *sermo familiaris* (Étude, p. 18). Prudentius follows the frequent usage of poets in using the nom. form for the *voc.;* cf. P. 2, 530; 3, 86; 4, 89; 10, 373; 834; A. 395, etc.; cf. also Priscillianus, 95, 8; *Dee* occurs in H. 931, elsewhere Deus, cf. C. 4, 81, etc. He uses the form *Persephone* in A. 475, and

---

¹ Schepss, Archiv, 3, 314; see further Neue, I, p. 29, and Georges Lex. Lat. Wortform.

⁹ Taken up also by Gregory of Tours; cf. Bonnet, p. 242, 24.

³ Goelzer, de la latinité de S. Jérôme, Par. 1884, p. 102.

⁴ Wölfflin, Archiv, 5, 497; also 7, 474, and Rhein. Mus. 37, 95. Gröber, Archiv, 1, 62.

⁶ Neue, Formenlehre II³, 469 (1892), does not cite any of these occurrences.

Proserpina in 13 lines below. *cuius*, a, um, the pron. rel. occurs
in Praef. 33;[1] the interrog. is frequent in Plaut. and Ter. (cf. also
Verg. Ecl. 3, 1 ; 5, 87 ; *cuias* (-atis) occurs in Ps. 708. *volupe*, P.
9, 41 ; the occurrence of such a form has been disputed.[2] Though
volup may be the correct form for Plaut. and Ter., volupe I regard
to be above dispute here. But Delbrück[3] remarks, "whether
the older form volupe is to be read in Plautus I am not able to
decide," and Reifferscheid, Arnob. 268, 19, says, "volupe scrip-
tum fuisse apparet," though he reads volup.[4] Georges, Lex. d.
lat. Wortformen, and Manitius, Rhein. Mus. 45 (1890) p. 491,
regard *volupe* as the reading of this passage.[5] It is the reading
of Obbarius, Arevalo and Dressel. For mage instead of magis,
cf. §128, note 1. *inpuratus*, P. 10, 191, an archaism ; Plaut. Rud.
751 ; cf. also Apul. 9, 10 ; Min. Fel. 23, 9.

§2. **Conjugation.** These forms may be noted : *fuant*, S. 1,
504 (fuat, Cl. Mar. Vict. Aleth. 1, 406); *adsies*, P. 2, 569 ; cf. siet
in Juv. 2, 40; Cl. Mam. 203, 7 ; *cluo* (for clueo), a rare word, observed only in Plautus, Accius, Seneca, Mart. Capella, Ausonius,
Symmachus, Ennodius, Ven. Fortunatus, and Prudentius who
uses it 4 times, C. 9, 107 ; Ps. 2 ; S. 1, 417 : cluis ; S. 2, 585 : cluat ;
cluis also used by Cypr. Gall., Ind. 237 ; *luiturus*, Ps. 535 (cf. luis
(nom.) H. 249 ; Ps. 508); *denseo*, C. 5, 53 ; H. 409 ; etc., an
archaism. *potesse*, P. 10, 803 ; cf. Lucr. 1, 666 ; *potis est*, S. 1, 331 ;
potis with esse occurs 11 times (with est 9 times, with es 2 times),
and always with negative sentences exc. Spr. 1, 84 ; not used without esse ; Vergil uses it 3 times and only in negative sentences
(Wotke). This archaic expression occurs frequently in Plautus,
there being almost 600 with an omission of esse ; Terence, however, employs esse.[6] Cf. potis est, Cypr. Gall. Numb. 291 ; 22
times in Arnobius. Prud. uses 16 forms in -*ier ;* of these, 10 are
in the hexameter poems ; 8 are in the 4th and 5th ft.; 2 in the 3d
and 4th ; only 2 out of the 16 forms were used before, dicier
(Plaut. and Pers.), spargier (Hor.), if the list in Neue, II², 409 is
complete. The list is given by Manitius[7] with the exception of

---

[1] Neue, Form. II³, p. 472, does not cite this example.
[2] Cf. Engelbrecht, Stud. Ter. p. 31. Buecheler, Grund. d. lat. Decl.² p. 11.
[3] Delbrück, Vergl. Synt., p. 603 (1893).
[4] Cf. also Stolz, Handb. d. Alterthumswiss. II², §69 ; Hist. Gram. (1894),
§189.
[5] See further Lindsay, The Latin Language. 1894, p. 205.
[6] Engelbrecht, Stud. Ter., p. 29.
[7] Rhein. Mus. 1890, p. 487.

negarier, P. 7, 54: such forms according to Riemann (Étude, p. 9) belong to the sermo vulgaris. Arnobius uses 11 such forms, (Neue, II², 409, gives but 6); Sedulius uses 3, none of which occur in Prudentius; *licitum est*, Ps. 692; S. 1, 337; an archaism (according to Wotke, Wien. Stud. 1886, 130) used by Verg. A. 10, 344; Juv. 4, 757; and Gell. 10, 15, 17. These also occur: *faxo*, Ps. 249; P. 10, 107; also in Petronius, Plautus and Terence; *ausim*, S. 1, 646; ausit, H. 47; P. 5, 414; *vagat*, for vagatur, C. 6, 29; used by Plautus, Pacuvius, Accius, and Ennius; also by Commod. instr. 1, 33, 1; *perarmat*, used only by Prud. C. 6, 86 and 7, 93 (Curtius, 4, 9, 6; 23; only in the form perarmatus).

§3. **Contracted Verb-Forms** (cf. Cic. Or. 47, 157; Quint. 1, 6, 17–21) occur: (a) *Indicative:* creasti, S. 1, 266; effigiasti, C. 10, 4; expiasti, P. 13, 61; norunt, P. 5, 85; optarunt, S. 2, 549; piarunt, S. 2, 678; sacrarunt, S. 2, 972; sprerunt, D. 123; mandaram, S. 2, 261; accumularat, Ps. 183; animarat, Ps. 37; audierat, Ps. 318; firmarat, S. 1, 66; fumarat, Ps. 808; levarat, Ps. 578; pararat, Ps. 874; sedarat, S. 1, 4; spectarat, S. 1, 207; variarat, Ps. 856; vastarat, S. 2, 701; consuerant, S. 1, 537; monstrarant, S. 1, 201. (b) *Subjunctive:* armarit, S. 1, 95; crearit, S. 2, 96; norit, S. 1, 543; P. 10, 887; novarit, S. 2, 311; putarit, S. 2, 163; raptarit, S. 2, 55; radiarint, S. 1, 485; signarint, S. 1, 596; nosset, P. 9, 34; S. 1, 21; obiectasset, Ps. 503. (c) *Infinitive:* consecrasse, S. 1, 565; conviolasse, Ps. 398; dampnasse, S. 1, 93; dicasse, S. 2, 365; habitasse, S. 2, 299; inlustrasse, S. 1, 553; inperitasse, S. 2, 421; personasse, Epil. 34; pugnasse, S. 2, 652; resignasse, S. 1, 92; revocasse, S. 1, 91; sedasse, Ps. 697; servasse, S. 2, 366; tractasse, S. 2, 418. Also: dito (divito), S. 2, 998; reposto, S. 2, 967.

A comparison of Prudentius with Juvencus and Vergil in their use of the *perf. ind. act. 3rd pl.* shows that while Prudentius is in bulk about 3 times as much as Juv., he has used practically the same number of these forms, and that in the use of -ere he falls much below Vergil. There are 72 occurrences in all, 39 being in -ere to 33 in -erunt, which gives for Prudentius, taking into consideration only the hexameter poems, 29 in -ere to 20 in -erunt, or 60 per cent. of the former to 40 per cent. of the latter. Prudentius does not use as many forms in -ere as Juv. by 10 per cent., and falls 22 per cent. below the Vergilian usage in the Aeneid (Wotke, Wien. Stud. 8). Claudianus also shows a strong preference for the forms in -ere, according to Birt, Archiv, 4, 592.

Prudentius uses 30 forms in -erunt not in Vergil, 20 in his hexameter poems not in Vergil.

Instead of -ris in 2nd pers. sing., -re, the older form,[1] characteristic of the sermo familiaris, occurs at least 16 times. Such forms were particularly frequent in Plautus, 170 out of 200 ending in -re (Engelbrecht, Stud. Ter. App. 88), while in Terence all, 56, end in -re. In Prudentius the forms balance each other, 18 in -ris, 18 in -re; of -re forms, 12 are in ind., 6 in subj.; of forms in -ris, 13 are in ind., 5 in subj.

II.—SYNTAX.

A. Simple Sentences.

1. Declarative Sentences.

a) The Subject.

§4. The Subject expressed in the First and Second Person.—The pronouns are not as a general thing expressed, unless to express emphasis or to give definiteness.

Emphasis: nos fatentes loquemur, C. 4, 100; nos vescimur, C. 5, 107; ipse ego sum, S. 2, 220; tu inlinis, C. 9, 35; vos celebrabitis, S. 1, 53; cf. also C. 9, 7; 10, 17; P. 1, 64; 5, 34; 10, 20.

Note. The emphatic expression *tute ipse* occurs in A. 674; P. 2, 261; 9, 69; 10, 957; a not infrequent expression in Plautus and Terence.[2] Other expressions may be noted here, se ipsum, A. 251; semet, P. 2, 20 (Cypr. Gall. Ex. 649); vosmet, A. 1080; egomet, H. 789; suopte,[3] S. 2, 474 (suapte, Priscill. 54, 15); sibimet, P. 12, 25; S. 1, 200; 2, 359; 440. Mihimet, S. 2, 265.

Antithesis: nos novimus, C. 2, 45; nos reddimus, C. 4, 75; sed nos mersimus, A. 217; ille vetuit, tu prohibeto, S. 2, 1125; ast ego feram, P. 3, 208; tu revehes, P. 4, 53; ego nescio, P. 10, 1000.

Less emphatic: not so common, nos intelleximus, A. 235; nos volumus, H. 559; tu extollis, P. 2, 201; cf. also P. 4, 193; 5, 25; 10, 585.

Note. A change in the number of the subject seems to occur in: nos date perluamus, ut absolvam, P. 4, 195; and possibly in: Ieiunamus, ait, recuso potum, P. 6, 54.

---

[1] Cf. Stolz, Hist. Gram. d. lat. Spr. I, §366 (1894).

[2] Verg. Ecl. 3, 35; for further examples cf. Georges, Lex. d. lat. Wortform., and Neue, Formenlehre.

[3] Cf. Luc. Mueller, De Re Metr.[2] (1894), p. 485.

§4a. **Impersonal Verbs**: vivitur, C. 2, 33; S. 2, 471, 610; itur, C. 7, 108; 10, 92; datur, C. 3, 192; creditur, S. 2, 504; exigitur, C. 3, 121; ventum erat, Ps. 665; ventum, A. 207; P. 2, 178; P. 5, 213; perventum, P. 10, 826; eundum est, P. 12, 26; dicendum, Pr. 31; luctandum, S. 2, 149; vigilandum, Pspr. 52; revolandum, H. 815; sudatum est, Ps. 820; iussum est, P. 6, 41.

Note. The impersonal verbs relating to natural occurrences do not seem to occur, but the following are worthy of note: arbor pluit, C. 3, 79; Dominus pluit, A. 316; cf. the Greek, Her. 2, 1, 13: ὁ θεὸς ὕει;[1] nubes verna pluit, S. 2, 788; imber pluit, P. 10, 1032. This use of *pluit*[2] has hitherto been observed only in Pliny (N. H.), Statius and Arnobius, according to Draeger, Hist. Synt.² §98. Other uses:

Roma erubuit, pudet, odit, S. 1, 512; and it ille nec pudet sequi, P. 2, 177; (this personal use of *pudet* is to be regarded as an archaism) virtutem nil vile decet, S. 2, 752; cf. flexus deceat miserationem, Quint. 1, 11, 12. A number of instances occur in Horace. *Paenitens* occurs in Pspr. 49; cf. also S. 1, 517: ubi videt paenitet, cupit; cf. paeniteo, S.² 48, 16, lat. Sirach (Archiv, 9 (1894) 253. *Est*=it is possible: visere est non, H. 82; cernere erat, A. 64, cf. Verg. Aen. 6, 596; 8, 676. For other occurrences cf. Wölfflin, Archiv, 2, 135; Hauler, 3, 537; Thielmann, 8, 260, 556.

b) **Predicate.**

a) IN GENERAL.

§5. **Present Participle with Copula**: this periphrasis occurring so frequently in Lucifer of Cagliari, Hartel citing about 75 examples of its use, appears but once in Juvencus (Hatfield), and but twice in Prudentius; unum erit gigneus, H. 43; and una via est errans, S. 2, 896 (?). Much more frequent, however, in the Vulgate N. T.; here, according to Milroy,[3] it occurs 138 times with esse.

Note: habere with perf. pass. part. occurs in S. 1, 211; persuasumque habuit. This usage was employed by Caesar, cf. 1, 9, 3; 15, 1, etc.

---

[1] Cf. also Aristoph. Nub. 368 and Kock's note (1894 ed.).

[2] Koffmane, Gesch. d. kirch. Lat., p. 117, on pluit in the sense of "permits to rain," cites its use in the Vulgate, in Tert., Arnob., August., and others; see also Am. Journ. Phil. XV (1894), p. 353.

[3] Milroy: The Participle in the Vulgate New Testament, Baltimore, 1892.

§6. Omission of Verb.

1) *Omission of forms of esse is* very common: certa fides, H. 922; nosse nefas, C. 3, 116; O beatus ortus ille, C. 9, 19; nam verbum Deus, C. 11, 24; summa quies, Ps. 609; nihil summum (est), H. 22; qui solus ac verus Deus, P. 5, 39; cf. also S. 1, 287, 477, 656; S. 2, 823; H. 330; P. 2, 429. Cf. also §4a.

Note: esse is often omitted when it constitutes part of the infinitive, as, negandum, C. 1, 52; prolapsum, C. 1, 58; velandam, A. 628; persuasum, S. 1, 283; relatos, P. 1, 96; reditura, A. 1081; cremandos, P. 6, 50, etc.

2) *Verb of saying:* Haec ubi legatus, S. 2, 17; martyr ad ista nihil, P. 3, 126; vix haec ille, P. 11, 89; ille sub haec, P. 13, 92. Such omissions are frequent in Juvencus (H.), though not occuring often in Prudentius; cf. also quid, quod veritas patet? P. 10, 231 ; quid, cum accipit? P. 10, 1076.

β) AGREEMENT.

In general the usual constructions are found, but it may be noted that when several subjects are joined asyndetically, the verb is usually in the plural, as e. g. Ps. 449, 464, and H. 358.

§7. Agreement of Number (cf. §4, note).

1) *Plural with Collectives:* pars conscendunt celeres, C. 5, 55; (cf. pars tergent, Aen. 7, 626). Both numbers occur in P. 11, 189; omnis adorat pubis, eunt, redeunt. The verb in subordinate clause is plural in P. 10, 83 ; inlitterata credidit frequentia ut se consecrandos autumnent, also P. 10, 697. The singular is more frequent, pars, H. 817; P. 9, 56; pubes, C. 5, 69 (but cf. 73); turba, C. 5, 53; 7, 152; P. 10, 80; grex, P. 10, 56: plebs, C. 5, 68; P. 5, 391; A. 330; iuventus, P. 14, 29.

2) *Predicate Verb in Singular after several subjects:* protervitas et luxus foedavit, Praef. 12; nemus et vernat coma, C. 8, 45; virginitas et fides bibit, A. 583; maiestas, bonitas et pietas tua continuat, C. 5, 163.

§8. Agreement of Gender.

1) *Masculine for Neuter.* Prudentius always uses the neuter with milia, as e. g. C. 9, 59; Juv. uses the masc. once, 1, 170 (H.).

2) *Masculine after Persons of different sexes:* Iocus et Petulantia primi, Ps. 433; this seems to be nearest approach to such a usage, and probably the only example.

γ) TENSES.

§9. The Historical Present is very common and, as in Juvencus, occurs more frequently than the past tenses in narration.

§10. Interchange of Tenses.

1) *Perf. Infin. for Pres.*: abesto procul ne libeat tetigisse quid, C. 3, 177; quis dixisse ausit, H. 45 (cf. Ov. Tr. 1, 5, 4); cf. Commod. 15, 11, amasse debuerat; Ennodius, 234, 5, debuit suscepisse; 365, 5, potuit intulisse.[1]

2) *Fut. Imperative for Pres.*: O Nazarene, adesto, C. 7, 3; cf. Adesto et percipe, P. 5, 545; also S. 1, pr. 84; S. 2, 1123.[2]

3) *A mixture of tenses sometimes occurs*, as of the historical present and perfect in: Roma erubuit, pudet, odit, S. 1, 512; ille agit et canit. Flevit Africa, P. 13, 96; dat poculum, fixum . . . . deinde monuit, C. 6, 61; cf. Claud. Mar. Vict. 3, 264.

Note. The pres. infin. for the future, frequent in Commodianus, does not seem to occur; but cf. Eugippius, 25, 2; promittentes se obviare; Ennod. 50, 16, remittere promisi.

§11. Present Subjunctive after a past tense: but few cases occur, perhaps only: stulta delegit Deus ut concidant sophistica, Apr. (2) 30, but with regular sequence in the foll. clause; (cf. Paul Ep. ad Cor. 1. 1, 27, ἐξελέξατο, and *elegit* of Vulgate, foll. by pres. both times, but by imp. in verse 28), percurrit arundo quadrent ut, Ps. 827; corpusque parens fecit ut possit, S. 2, 259; iussit ne quis adoret, Commod. 1, 8, 7.

§12. Tenere with almost the force of an auxiliary verb occurs 3 times in Juvencus according to Hatfield; I have found but two cases in Prudentius that are at all similar: quem gaza dives ac triumphus impeditum tenebant, Pspr. 25, and quo corda hominum coniuncta teneret amor, S. 2, 590, cf. the Spanish, *tener*; this usage occurs also in Cicero.[3]

§13. Gnomic Perfect. A few cases occur: Felix qui meruit visere principem, C. 5, 33; voluit Pater ipse coniectare, H. 82; Felix qui potuit uti, H. 330; felices animae quibus contigit, P. 6, 98. The present also occurs, though neither frequently.

[1] See further, Howard, The Perfect Infinitive with the Force of the Present, Harv. Stud. 1, p. 122 (1890).

[2] Forms in *-to* are frequent in Plaut., Riemann, Rev. d. Phil. 10 (1886), p. 161.

[3] Thielmann, Archiv, 2, 403.

δ) Moods.

1. *Subjunctive.*

§14. **Optative,** generally without utinam; once with utinam: O utinam corporis emicem liber, Praef. 44.

§15. **Potential.**

a) Auae tuba aequiperare queat? C. 3, 85; in rhetorical questions frequently: C. 5, 30; 8, 50; Apr. (2) 17, 631, 672, 850, 939; H. 230; S. 1, 79, 267, 271; 2, 101; P. 1, 112, etc.; in direct statements: ausim, H. 80; S. 1, 646; deponas velim, S. 1, 499; 2, 270; P. 2, 169; 11, 234; discas, A. 834; putares, P. 6, 109.

(With an indefinite subject in 2nd person: videas, C. 5, 79; audias, P. 1, 103; credas, P. 4, 73; C. 5, 145; and videres, P. 2, 281; cerneres, C. 9, 100; P. 5, 334.)

b) Aoristic perf. = pres. is rare: crediderim aliquem se dixisse deum, S. 1, 176.

§16. **Jussive.** Frequent, as, agnoscat Iudaea legens, A. 384; frenentur ergo cupidines, C. 7, 21; nemo accuset, H. 524; te volvant, Ps. 94, cf. also S. 2, 289; P. 10, 116; Pr. 38, etc.

2. *Imperative.*

§17. **The Future is used for the Imperative** in: ignibus vorabere et fies, P. 10, 815. This occurs much more frequently in Juvencus. Cf. also, vade et dices, Vict. Vit. 42, 24. Used already by Horace, cf. S. 1, 1, 16; 105.

§18. Imperative correlated with **Jussive Subj.**: terge neve tingat, C. 8, 25; psallat, psallite, C. 9, 22; occidat scrutare, C. 12, 101; elige rem vitae, tua virtus provehat, H. 705; ebibe cruorem, sint haec tibi, Ps. 428; abscide caput, crux istum tollat, P. 11, 65; cf. also P. 1, 119; 4, 150; 9, 37, etc.

§19. **Other uses.** a) particularly of *age, fac,* etc.: age explicemus, P. 10, 168; dic age, H. 108; (Hor. O. 1, 32, 4; 2, 11, 22) fare age, A. 129 (cf. Aen. 6, 389); age, adure, seca, divide, P. 3, 91; cf. surge age, Aen. 10, 241; fac figura signet, C. 6, 132, a colloquialism, cf. fac memineris, Claud. Mam. 205, 19; but fac ut, P. 10, 4; 518; 655; etc. The old imperative form *cedo* occurs; ipsa mater adsit cedo, P. 10, 686; and in Hoc iam cedo, P. 7, 83. Cf. §93.

b) **Imperative in Prohibitions**: two instances: ne tollito, Ps. 613; ne trepidate, Ps. 624; this is a vulgarism, Riemann, Ét. p. 259 (Servius ad Aen. 6, 544 considers such usages archaic).

Cf. Ter. Phorm. 803; Hor. C. 1, 28, 23. Elsewhere is used : nolite
quaerere, P. 10, 19; cf. Priap. 44, 1; cave velis, P. 10, 136[1] (cf. Hor.
S. 2, 3, 38; 2, 5, 75; Petron. S. §58) but cave fingere, S. 1, 497;
cf. cave deprimere, Commod. 2, 22, 8; vita orare, P. 10, 423.
The above are the only prohibitive phrases in Prudentius, ne with
pres. or perf. subj. not occurring.

3. Infinitive.

§20. **Historical Infinitive.** Here Juvencus has but 2 examples
and each begins with ecce; I have noticed 6 sentences, 13 verbs, in
Prud.: Perfidus ille caput curvare, lambere, advolvi, incerare, A.
455; spernere sucina, flare rosas, P. 3, 21; Trepidare carnifex, P.
10, 861; lorea stridere, virgarum concrepitare fragor, P. 11, 56;
ungula altos pandere secessus et lacerare iecur, P. 11, 58; ipse
modesta loqui, spem quaerere, P. 13, 31. This construction occurs
7 times in Paulinus Petricordiae, and 3 times in Cl. Mar. Victor in
the Alethia; according to Trump[2] it occurs frequently in Claudianus.

§21. **Infinitive as Substantive**: Nasci suum, H. 173; id
ipsum gignere, A. 260; cf. hoc ipsum venire, Faust. Rei. 47, 19;
hoc esse, Cl. Mar. Vict. 1, 45; simplex ut esset credere, Apr. 32 (?);
sit difficilis via noscere, A. 264; gloria est calcare et sistere, P. 7, 59;
genus mortis donare, P. 1, 27, and cf. Ps. 159; cedo hoc pro te
mori, P. 7, 85; Christum hausi credere, P. 10, 685; habet munus
divinitas reddere, P. 10, 953; hoc sequimur, adpellare Patrem, A.
240; cf. also S. 1, 22; 311; P. 5, 386, and P. 10, 59. Cf. spes,
suberat gaudera, Cl. Mar. Vict., Aleth. 2, 206.

Note. For the infinitive after necesse est, etc., see §98; after
adjs., §60 note.

§22. **The Infinitive in exclamations** does not occur in
Juvencus according to Hatfield, but it occurs in Prudentius as
follows: ingenuas naturae occumbere leges, ceptivas trahi dotes!
H. 304; Tene potuisse recalescere! Ps. 58; vos non potesse dissipare! P. 10, 803; cf. also, Quid verbum posse videri? A. 44.

ε) VOICE.

§23. **Personal Passive from Intransitives.** But two cases
have been cited in Juv., and no clear cases have been found in
Prudentius.

---

[1] "Plautus and Terence present 33 instances of cave with perfect, 18 with
the present." Elmer, Am. Journ. Phil. XV (1894), p. 142.
[2] F. Trump, Observ. ad Genus Dicendi Claudiani, p. 37.

§24. **Active for Passive.** Here, as above, but two have been cited in Juvencus, and none found in Prudentius.

§25. **Juror as Deponent Verb.** A possible case occurs in S. 2, 697: Geticus iuratus has arces aequare, though Dressel's punctuation is against it. It occurred in Plaut. Amph. 437 ; As. 23 ; also in Juvencus, 3, 60.

§26. **Deponent Participle with Middle Signification.** *Conversus* seems to be the only verb thus used, and thus used but twice : nec sol potis est conversus iter revocare, S. 1, 333 ; also P. 2, 183; Hieronymus on the other hand very frequently employs deponent participles in a passive sense (Goelzer, St. Jer. p. 351). *Versus* seems to be used thus in D. 96. *Note :* accingere with middle signification occurs in P. 10, 421 ; a not infrequent usage of Comedy.[1]

c) **Attribute.**

§27. **Substantive as Attribute.** Frequent : sermo Christe et Spiritus, C. 6, 3 ; Christe regimen, C. 8, 1 ; puer redemptor protulit, C. 9, 21 ; Moyses receptor, C. 12, 144; quem sacerdotem adsumpsit, C. 12, 154; Christus ultor, A. 409; draco victor, Ditt. 4 ; domini Christi, H. 621 ; fratrum ducum, S. 2, 17 ; fama proditrix, P. 1, 11 ; cygnus stuprator, P. 10, 221 ; ab urbe Roma, P. 10, 408; cf. also C. 12, 43; A. 609, 893; H. 577, 622; Pspr. 2, 345, 805; P. 2, 30, 180, 465 ; 4, 18, 37 ; 10, 615, 635, 835 ; etc. Not infrequently joined asyndetically : quisque gerat, miles, togatus navita, opifex, arator, institor, C. 2, 38 ; cf. also C. 12, 197 ; H. 395; P. 6, 148; 10, 970; 14, 106.

§28. **Attributive use of Adverb.** It is believed that no cases of this occur in Prudentius ; such a usage occurs 8 times in Lucifer Cal., cf. also Paul. Pell. 24 and 576; also Cyprian, De Zelo, 18.

d) **Apposition.**

§29. **Paratactic Apposition.** A case similar to that found in Juvencus of pocula vinum, 4, 658, is believed not to occur in Prudentius.

§30. **Apposition to Sentence** : quocunque modo sit factus, id unus scit, A. 893 ; populare quiddam credidit frequentia ut autumnent, P. 10, 82.

§31. **Apposition to Pronoun unexpressed** : victor adscendit, C. 9, 104 ; rex serenus aspice, C. 7, 4 ; martyr cerno, P. 11, 34; ut comes sequatur, P. 13, 48; si martyr insilias, Ps. 775.

---

[1] Holtze, Syntaxis pris. script. lat. 2, p. 20.

e) Cases.

1. NOMINATIVE.

§32. Nominative with proh in Exclamations : Pro Jupiter, P. 10, 396; cf. Ter. Andr. 732, etc.; proh pudor, Ps. 353; P. 5, 129; in Oros. 337, 14; pro caeca libido, H. 628; pro dolor, H. 304; cf. pro dolor in Claud. in Ruf. 1, 55; 2, 214; in Sedul. 2, 9; in Paul. Petr. 3, 377; in Oros. 223, 19; pro labor, Claud. Bell. Gild. 1, 94. Cf. also §40.

2. ACCUSATIVE.

§33. After Verbs of Motion: domum vexit, S. 2, 351; domum referre, P. 6, 133; domum revertor, P. 9, 106; 12, 65; all in conformity with the classical usage.

But it may be noticed that Hier. frequently uses ad with names of towns : in patriam' scandere occurs in C. 5, 112; remeasse ad superos, C. 3, 200. Usque is used in, usque pervenitis rivulum, P. 10, 160. (penetrare chaos, S. 2, 903; penetrare gremium, S. 1, 78; 10 occurrences of penetrare with acc. have been noticed; Juvencus used the same construction 8 times (Marold. p. 115). Like Juv., Prud. also uses in and per with this verb, as in H. 319, Ps. 677).

§34. Transitive Accusative.

1) *After Verbs compounded with prepositions:* aram adit, Ps. 844; tribunal adit, P. 3, 64; recessus circumibat tortiles, C. 7, 124; increpat vitium, Ps. 284; cf. C. 7, 132; 9, 37; A. 657; incidit occurs with in, Ps. 533 (decidet in, Juv. 3, 158; though he also uses simple acc. with incido in 2, 2, and 589); caelum percurrere, A. 806; cf. P. 12, 21; praecucurrit filium, C. 7, 47; praestare (to show, to furnish) with acc., A. 81; H. 49; 667; C. 9, 50; P. 2, 32; 3, 55; 5, 516, 527; 10, 124; 11, 75; palatum praeterit, C. 7, 120; sensum doloris mors praevenit, P. 14, 90; cf. P. 10, 71; os omne transit, C. 7, 120; incruentam transvolans linguam, C. 7, 117; invadit (eam) trepidam, Ps. 589; incurrit id, Apr. (2) 38; also with in, S. 2, 1029; (pectori insedit suo, P. 10, 461); locum invenit, C. 12, 113; membrum invenerit, C. 2, 90; (succedit illis, P. 10, 1103, but acc. in Livy, 22, 28, 12); incubare, cf. §54.

2) Other Verbs: *mentita* sociam figuram, Ps. 684; lupus lacteolam mentitus ovem, Ps. 792; sudavit proelium, C. 2, 76.

¹ This may be added to the passage in Val. Max. cited by Wölfflin, Archiv, 7 (1892), p. 582.

§35. **Duration of Time**, with a preposition: quos per omne tempus iunxerat, P. 1, 53; meruit ter quinque per annos proferre diem, Ditt. 93. Without a preposition: none. For the abl. to express duration of time cf. §71, note; the ablative seems to be his favorite case, rather than the acc.

§36. **Cognate Accusative**: (This has been regarded as an archaism, cf. Kühnast, Liv. Synt. p. 141; it occurs, however, frequently in the letters of Cicero and in Comedy.) vivere iustitiam, P. 13, 32; quod sumus et quod vivimus, S. 2, 121; nec doleas quia turpe tibi gemuisse dolorem, Ps. 120; quae vivendo, S. 2, 660.

§37. **Accusative of Specification.** 21 occurrences:

a) 19 refer to some part of the body, as: nuda humeros, Ps. 23; defixa oculos, Ps. 112; tempora redimitus, H. 498 (cf. Aen. 3, 81); distenta uterum, H. 585.

b) The two referring to the mind are, mentem purgata, S. 2, 323; animum recisum castrata, H. 957. The remaining occurrences of the former (a) are: Ps. 312; S. 1, 235, 492; two more in Ps. 23; H. 965; C. 3, 30; C. 8, 38; P. 4, 13, 55; 10, 353; 14, 41; also vincitur manus, P. 9, 43; tundatur terga, P. 10, 116. Here may be noticed, faces succincta, Ps. 42. (With this participle, only by Ovid, says Draeger, Hist. Synt.[1] §166, B.)

§38. **The Accusative after the passive of a verb of clothing**, very rare: papillas vestita, S. 2, 38; (exutus occurs with *abl.* in A. 428).

§39. **Two Accusatives**, very rare; with infin. as second acc.: docuit colonos servire, S. 1, 85.

§40. **Accusative of Exclamation.** 8 cases: O linguam, S. 1, 632; O miraclum, C. 9, 85; O tenerum animum, S. 2, 1096; O novum saporem, P. 13, 11; en Christum, A. 503; en documentum, H. 769; en nummos, P. 2, 293; ecce duas dotes, P. 12, 55; ecce also with the dat. cf. §56, c.

3. Genitive.

§41. **Appositional Genitive.** Prudentius shows a marked fondness for this use of the genitive. Hatfield points out a similar characteristic in Juvencus. The following may be noted: mole praedarum, Pspr. 27; trinitas angelorum, Pspr. 45; frusta auri, Ps. 588; pluviam auri, S. 1, 68; vis animi, S. 2, 25; generisque propagine, S. 2, 224; Almonis rivulum, P. 10, 160; res naturae, S. 2, 803; vitium sceleris, H. 642, etc. With a word denoting place, urbibus Sodomae et Gomorrhae, Pspr. 17; littoris acta, S. 1, 136; regione plagae, S. 2, 613.

After *nomen:* nomen Christi, S. 1, 494; A. 403; P. 5, 91; Triviae nomine, S. 1, 371; nomen Israel, C. 12, 95; (or acc.? cf. 160, and Israelis, P. 1, 40); nomen Patris supremi, P. 13, 54; A. 240; Martyris nomen, P. 11, 8; but cf. loco Latium dabo nomen, S. 1, 48.

Note. For constructions after nomen est, etc., cf. §55.

§42. **Objective Genitive,** common: cupido rerum, C. 6, 120; laudis amorem, Ps. 279; deditionis amorem, Ps. 340; amore deorum, S. 2, 1068; sitis sanguinis, H. 396; cf. also Ps. 233, 445, 607; S. 1, 99, 341, 406, 618; H. 554, 621; dilectio nostri, A. 1027.

§43. **Genitive after Verbal Nouns in -tor and -trix.** A number of cases occur: dator vitae, Ps. 624; dissipator triumphi, Pspr. 34; auctorem sui, Pspr. 42; moderator orbis, S. 1, 9; arator ruris, S. 2, 937; also S. 1, 625; S. 2, 435; H. 566, 641; in -trix: ostentatrix splendoris, Ps. 439; victrix orbis, Ps. 480; also Ps. 587, 630, 668, 681, etc.

§44. **Genitive of Quality,** not frequent: vir severae industriae, C. 7, 67; senem perversi dogmatis olim, P. 11, 23; corporis formam caduci, C. 9, 16; insignis auri lammina, P. 10, 1084; nostri (pl.) decoris integri, P. 2, 226; decem saxorum pagina, Ditt. 38; aliquem generosae stirpis, S. 1, 170; alter externi generis, H. 49; amictum pietatis, S. 1, 546; stirpem gentis patriciae, S. 1, 560. Expression of *name:* Olybriaci nominis haeres, S. 1, 554.

This gen. is very frequent in Hier. and used with adjs. (Goelzer, Hier. p. 318).

§45. **Partitive Genitive.**

1) *With numerals:* milia pugnarum, Ps. 168; milia virorum, Ps. 481; also S. 1, 516; S. 2, 448; H. 95, 413; C. 11, 29; P. 2, 76; Ditt. 146; una gentis, Ps. 502 (cf. Livy, 21, 63, 3); but cf. de grege, A. 291; P. 10, 662 (cf. Hor. O. 3, 11, 33; Caes. B. G. 1, 32, 2; St. Aug. 266, §4); with ex: P. 10, 767; also Petron. §57. Solus e cunctis, C. 7, 111, (nullus ex famulis, P. 11, 61).

2) *With neuter pronouns:* quodcunque temporis, C. 1, 78; quidquid gentium, C. 12, 201; quocunque loci, A. 118; quidquam mentis, C. 11, 95; quodque laudis, S. 2, 1123; cf. also S. 1, 3; 2, 366; H. 582; P. 2, 65; 431; 513.

3). *With substantivized neuter adjectives,* (for a list cf. §120).

a). *In the singular* is rare: tantum peccati, H. 153; auxilii, H. 467; medelae, S. 1, 526; C. 7, 192. arcanum rerum, S. 2, 75; summo pontis, P. 7, 21. This is an essentially poetical construction.

b) *In the plural* is more common: infima terrae, H. 517; pectoris abdita, H. 537; summa fluctuum, C. 9, 49; frivola famae, Ps. 231; per extima calcis, Ps. 653; super ardua caeli, S. 1, 148; in ardua famae, S. 1, 281; sancta sanctorum, Ps. 815; suavia fluxae conditionis, S. 2, 150; also Praef. 40; C. 2, 2; cf. contigua terrae, Cl. Mam. 144, 17.

Note. The abl. with de occurs in: nil de pestiferis opibus, H. 549; with ex: nihil ex septem septenis, A. 992.

4) *With substantivized adjectives used personally:* nulla linguarum, C. 9, 24; nulla avium, Ps. 617; maxima furiarum, Ps. 96; (primus e septem viris, P. 2, 37; cf. Act. Apost. 6, 3).

5) *After pronouns used personally:* quis sapientum, S. 2, 403; quisque hominum, A. 22; quis perfidorum, P. 5, 413; ecquis virorum, P. 5, 449; quidam militum, P. 5, 465; but with de in H. 167, and P. 6, 52 (ex in Gell. 12, 6, 11); aliquem de gente, H. 946.

§46. Predicate Genitive with esse: Sapientiae est, S. 1, pr. 46; omnipotentiae est, S. 2, pr. 46; difficilis operis fuit, S. 2, 527; hominis, Dei est, H. 665; (esse) operis tui, S. 1, pr. 82; also Apr. (1) 7; 559.

§47. Genitive with Adjectives of Relation. The following are considered worthy of note: liber, C. 1, 47 : P. 10, 657; but abl. cf. §70, note 2; egenus, Ps. 819; S. 1, 81; 377; C. 10, 82; A. 423; inpos mentis, C. 9, 53; Ps. 585; cf. Lact. de Ira Dei, 21, 3; vernularum divites, Pspr. 56; but abl. in P. 2, 108 (Horace uses abl.); vacuus cruoris, P. 4, 86. Hitherto observed only in Sall., Hor., Ov., and Tac. (Draeger, Hist. Synt.[1] §206), but cf. also Claud. Mam. Grat. act. ad Jul. 14; plena angelorum, P. 4, 5; plenum virtutis, Ps. 769; but plenus Deo, Pspr. 26; invidus unitatis, Hpr. 48; but dat. in Hor. Ep. 1, 15, 7; laris exul aviti, S. 2, 735 (poetical and p. A.); crucis peritus, P. 5, 254; securus tui, P. 5, 286; expertem prolis, Pspr. 65; S. 1, 86; C. 11, 15; P. 2, 228; 5, 246; avidus vini, S. 1, 126; fontem chrismatis feracem, P. 12, 34; Christi capaces, P. 2, 376; virtutum, P. 10, 743; (Draeger cites only Livy, Vell. and Plin.; he does not cite incapax at all: cf. scio incapacem te sacramenti, P. 10, 588); exors dolorum tristium, P. 5, 160, A. 898; Ps. 115; potens occurs with ad oppugnanda ludibria, Ps. 17 (poet. and p. A.). On *plenus*, etc., cf. also §68, note; on *similis*, cf. §60.

§48. Genitive of Charge or Penalty: crimine pietatis, H. 597; reus capitalis criminis, S. 2, 805; reus furti, Ditt. 27; (so reus voti, Aen. 5, 237) rea criminis, H. 713; paenam capitis, P. 13, 36.

§49. Genitive of Price or Value:[1] est tanti, H. 652; parvi pendo, P. 10, 478; magni putas, P. 2, 202; magni refert, P. 10, 119; flocci fecero, P. 10, 140; (note: Harper's Lat. Dict. marks this use of flocci ante-class.). Cf. also §63.

§50. Genitive Dependent on Genitive is very rare. Orphae fanorum ritus, H. 782; cuius omnipotentiae est, Spr. 2, 26; sanguinis pretium Christi, Ditt. 155.

§51. Genitive after Verbs of Remembering or Forgetting: meminisse pudoris, S. 1, 163; patriae, H. 460; memento matris, P. 10,835; oblita lactis, P. 10,738; Pr. 24; C. 1, 36; 7, 57; A. 501; H. 376. Acc. not used after these verbs.

§52. For the Genitive with Verbs of Plenty and Want see §68.

a) *Other Genitives.*

1) *Genitive with Comparatives.* This occurs independently of translations in unusually large numbers in African latinity.[2] It occurs in Symmachus, Ep. 11, 52, and Isid. Or. 17, 7, 52. There are a few phrases in Prudentius which may be noticed under this heading: (1) Magnarum urbium maior, C. 12, 77; (2) fortissimorum fortior, P. 5, 294; (3) quod malorum est taetrius omnium, P. 14, 110; (4) magnus qui discipulorum, Ps. 530. Of these (3) is very similar to Apul. dogm. Plat. 1, 9, omnium gignentium seniorem, though it may be explained as Ennius, Frag. 41, melior mulierum, in which, as Sittl remarks, the comparative stands in place of a superlative (cf. p. 114). With No. (1) cf. Sid. Apoll. Carm. 11, 52, magnorum maior avorum; (4) is equal to Aen. 4, 576, and Iliad 18, 205, and elsewhere, where the positive stands for a superlative; cf. Claud. Mam. 19, 4; 177, 1; Paul. Pell. 308, 314. Positive for comparative, Claud. Mam. 205, 21. The comp. is used 18 times in Paul. Petr. for the pos. or superl., cf. Commod. A. 659; 787. Comp. for pos. very frequent in Faust. Rei., 16 times in Ioh. Cass.; comp. for superl., omnium potior, Claud. Mam. 205, 1; Sedul. 185, 17; 240, 4; 5 times in Vict. Vit.; 5 times in Ioh. Cassianus; 21 times in Eugippius; Faust. Rei. 450, 17. Superl. is used for comp., Sedul. 12, 1. Accordingly we would regard all of the above four passages, not as

---

[1] The "Genitiv des Wertes," cf. Wölfflin, Archiv IX (1894), p. 101 et seq., Der Genitiv des Wertes und der Ablativ des Preises.

[2] Cf. Sittl, lok. Versch. d. lat. Spr., p. 114.

examples of genitives following comparatives, etc., but of positives and comparatives used for superlatives.[1]

Note 1. A phenomenon somewhat similar to the above appears in the Latin translation of the Book Sirach, in which Greek comparatives are translated by Latin positives, Gk. superl. by Lat. pos., etc. (Thielmann, Archiv, 8 (1893), pp. 246, 515).

Note 2. *a* or *ab* with ablative after comparatives, a construction appearing in Ambrose, Hieronymus and others, does not occur in Prudentius.

2) *Genitive with verbs of feeling* occurs in: miserando inopum, Ps. 580; but acc. Ps. 1; P. 2, 412. paenitens Cachinni, Pspr. 49; Roma pudet exacti temporis, S. 1, 512; miserescito huius, Spr. 1, 84.

3) *Frugi*, a form which Riemann[2] regards genetically as a genitive, and which Delbrück[3] and Lindsay[4] are inclined to regard rather as a dative,[5] occurs twice in Prudentius and seems to have in one passage the force of an adverb: sed nec magno opus est frugi viventibus, S. 2, 1015, where it = abstinenter, and in the other it may be translated as a noun: quam memorant frugi, parce cui vivere cordi est, Ps. 554.

4. DATIVE.

§53. **With Intransitives**: haerere, H. 851; S. 1, 173; P. 4, 41; inperare, A. 140; inperitare, C. 3, 162; S. 1, 368; cedere, S. 1, 633; suadere, H. 715; parcere, H. 937; Ps. 392; placere, Ps. 356; S. 1, 576; credere, A. 878; servire, H. 508, 680; iubere, A. 658; also used with acc. and infin., or with ut, cf. §99. (Here may be noted, sibi peccans, H. 742, cf. Deut. 1, 41; Reg. 2, 12, 13.)

Note. Comitari, which has the dative twice in Juv. and acc. once, has only the acc. in Prud., C. 10, 44; H. 779; Ps. 802; the Vergilian usage, G. 1, 346; A. 6, 112, etc.

§54. **After Verbs compounded with Prepositions.**

a) *Intransitives:* adesse, adsuescere, advolare (Aen. 10, 510), congredi (P. 10, 606), conpetere, constare, contingere, deesse,

---

[1] Wölfflin, Archiv, 7 (1892), p. 118, cites Nos. (2) and (3), explaining them as either genitives of comparison or examples of comparatives used for superlatives.

[2] Riemann, Revue de Phil., 1890, p. 66.

[3] Delbrück, Vergl. Gram. (1893), p. 409.

[4] Lindsay, Latin Lang. (1894), p. 407.

[5] Wölfflin, Archiv, IX (1894), p. 105, after frugi places "(Genitiv or Dativ?)."

incumbere, inesse, inscribere (with in and abl. in Cic. Cat. 1, 13, 32), insistere, instare, intervenire, obludere (H. 6, first by Prudentius), obtemperare, obsequi, obsistere, obstare, praecellere, praeludere, praesidere, resistere, restare, subesse, subire, subiacere, succedere, succumbere, succurrere, sufficere, superesse, superstare. *Note.* Incubare foll. by acc. in Juv. has dat. in H. 59; for praestare foll. by acc. cf. §34.

b) *Transitive Verbs*, which may also have a direct object in the accusative : abdere, addere, addicere, adsignare, circumdare, circumferre, conferre, coniungere, conponere, conserere, indere, indulgere (H. 799; Juv. has the dat. simply; cf. Caes. B. G. 7, 40), inferre, infundere, interfundere (S. 2, 380; I have found no parallel passage), inmiscere, inpertire, inponere, instituere, obicere, obiectare, obtendere, offerre, praescribere, subdere, subicere, subiungere, submittere, suspendere (inducere has the acc., cf. H. 50).

§55. **Nomen est.** I have noted but one occurrence of this expression : Eumorphio nomen fuit, P. 5, 466 (Eumorphio is regarded as a nom. by the author of the Delphin Ed., but De Vit in his Onomasticon gives Eumorphius as the nom.), more frequent in Juv. The dat. is used in Firm. Mat. 6, 1; cui Iunoni fuit nomen, and is the usual construction with Gregory of Tours, cf. Bonnet, p. 544. (Cognomento Heresis occurs in Ps. 710.)

§56. **Dative of Reference** (commodi et incommodi). These are common and may be divided into : (a) *Dativus energicus*[1]: homini, S. 2, 207; quibus, Ps. 56, etc., frequent.

b) *Commodi :* sibi, H. 172; Ps. 529, 720; S. 1, 299; 2, 348, 566; ipsi, H. 547; spiritibus, H. 841; Christo, S. 2, 620; tibi, S. 1, 265, 497; 2, 1120; cui, S. 1, 380; 2, 764; quibus, Ps. 56.

c) *Ethicus :* mihi, S. 2, 445, 659; C. 3, 71; A. 1046; en tibi, A. 503; H. 769; Ps. 118; P. 11, 69; ecce tibi, A. 340; etc. (cf. ecce tibi, Claud. Mam. 74, 7; 145, 6).

Note. With present participles : it is believed none occur in Prud.; Hatfield cites 4 for Juv., and it may be noted that 2 of these, surgenti, 1, 355, revertenti, 2, 76, contravene the statement of Landgraf, at bottom of page 53 of same article, who says that this construction does not occur at all in poetry after the Augustan Age.[2]

---

[1] Landgraf, Archiv, 8 (1893), p. 40.

[2] Landgraf: "Seltener ist er bei den Augusteischen Dichtern, und gar nicht findet er sich bei den Dichtern der folgenden Zeit. Vgl. Note 549 to Keisig's Vorles. und Wölfflin, Act. Erlang, II. 140."

Dative after verbs of deprivation and separation : palmam victoribus aufert, S. 2, 555; aliquid sibi detrahit, A. 277 (P. 6, 75; S. 2, 553); cui nulla recedi pars potest, S. 2, 238 ; vincula demam gregibus, S. 2,733; palmam sibi praeripi, P. 7, 52; noteworthy is, ovem gregi perditam sano, C. 8, 33.

§57. **Final Dative** used absolutely is rare : venere auxilio, S. 2, 536; indicio est annona, S. 2, 953; dis Manibus marmora lego, S. 1, 403; quae sunt odori, quaeque vernant esui, P. 10, 335; praesidio Christus adsit, Ps. 910; lapis nostro fixus offensaculo est, Apr. 33; locus Emerita est tumulo, P. 3, 186. With another dative : prosilit auxilio sociis, Ps. 574; sit lapidatio fraudi hostibus, Ditt. 179; neaerae non fuit ludibrio, P. 10, 240; numen adserentibus nihil pavori est, P. 10, 390.

Note. For the Final Dative after gerundive, see Gerundives, §83.

§58. **Dative after Passive Verbs**: a) After the gerundive invariably : Christo regendos, S. 1, 565; restituendus mihimet, S. 2, 265; avibus edendam, S. 2, 1049; bibendus tibi, P. 10, 736; cf. C. 3, 84; P. 10, 417; S. 2, 170; P. 5, 88.

b) After forms of the passive containing the perfect participle : dictus parenti, Pspr. 4; comitata viro, Ps. 163; angelico comitata choro, P. 3, 48; repulsa Deo, Ps. 900; Deo disposita, S. 1, 287; tibi parata, S. 2, 65; Christo perempta vero, C. 9, 112; imago nulli visa, A. 7; vim cunctis petitam, P. 14, 103.

c) After other passive forms, rare : nobis colitur, P. 10, 952; fit deus Indis, S. 1, 122; tibi soli calcentur, P. 5, 105.

§59. **Final Locative after Verbs of Motion.** This category has been denied for the Latin by Delbrück (Vergl. Synt. p. 290), who cannot regard the examples commonly adduced as "finale Lokale." Prudentius has used the following : caelo revolandum (est), H. 815; caelo refusus subvolabit spiritus, P. 10, 533; caelo reportans gloriam, C. 9, 105; venisse terris nuntiat Deum, C. 12, 7; tenebris mergitur, P. 10, 473; hominem portaret Patri, C. 11, 48; occisus redeat superis, A. 1059; qui sit dampnandus averno, H. 128 (and cf. Ps. 496); quosdam astris dampnavit, S. 2, 999;[1] sepulcro condita est, P. 10, 525; cf. Ps. 105, condere vaginae gladium; C. 10, 76, dedit ossa sepulcro ; agmina superis inmittere, S. 1, 362; also, messes deferre campo, Cypr. Gall. Gen. 1164;

---

[1] Cf. dampnasse neci, S. 1, 93; condemnare morti in S. Jerome, Goelzer, Étude, p. 315.

caelo redire, Commod. 1, 3, 5; cf. also Paul. Pell. 45; caelo ferunt Ambrosium, Eunod. C. 1, 15, 1.

§60. **Dative after Adjectives**: (conscius, used with dat. in Juv., is used with gen. in Prud., H. 598; Ps. 703; P. 5, 223; P. 13, 52; Oros. 4, 9, 4; cf. also noctis mihi conscius, Spr. 2, 52. nescius also occurs with gen.: S. 2, 875; P. 5, 234; C. 2, 46; 5, 757; 9, 64; 10, 79; so also praescius, Ps. 260, and inscius, S. 2, 1131; C. 3, 75; A. 575). Proprius, utilis, aptus, carus, dispar, inpar are foll. by dat.; communis cunctis viventibus, S. 2, 86; membra morti obnoxica, C. 9, 16; miserae postuma matri, H. 607; proximus occiduo, P. 3, 6; proxima dotibus, P. 3, 110; secto proximum, P. 5, 524; (also proximus ad aram, P. 2, 38). Similis, as in Horace, occurs both with the gen. and with the dat.; with the former: A. 797, similis Dei, and 799, sui similem, but in 790 the latter is used, similis creanti; in 807, his similem (these are believed to be the only occurrences); simillimus austro, A. 611; adsimilis vento, A. 954; cf. similis deo, Claud. Mam. 97, 8. Here may be noted angusta lobori, S. 2, 98.

Note 1. *Studiosa* occurs in P. 4, 54, with Christi, though Obbarius following some of the MSS has the dat. Christo; Faguet, p. 96, also regards the dat. the better reading. But a dat. with studiosus occurs only in Plautus, Mgl. 802, according to Brix and Lorenz, ad loc.[1]

Note 2. *The infinitive after adjectives:* contenti vesci, A. 711; also H. 382; Ps. 105; S. 2, 346; P. 11, 44; Spr. 1, 54; Draeger, §434, 3, cites Ovid as the only poet to use it, but Juvencus uses it in 3, 619, and Paulinus Pell., Euch. 190 has contentus exercere; cf. also §67; certa mori, Ps. 586; suetus vivere, C. 5, 39; suetus dare, C. 7, 70; also C. 9, 52; S. 1, 106; P. 10, 886; adsuetos ali, P. 2, 158; diffundere promptus, Apr. (1) 11, concurrere promptum, A. 19, (Draeger cites no use of promptus); abolere paratus, C. 10, 18; cf. S. 2, 865; P. 1, 54; 2, 112; 5, 415; cf. paratus curare, Sedul. 4, 182; peritus pellere, P. 5, 450; conprendere, P. 9, 23; vertere, P. 10, 870. potens mutare, Ditt. 192, urere potens, P. 13, 79, (Draeger cites only Manil. and Sil.); facilis conprendier, A. 7; flecti, Spr. 1, 27; rapi, H. 429 (not in Vergil and Horace, Draeg.); dignus subire, P. 10, 99; cf. P. 10, 205; Ps. 497, (Huemer cites 10 examples from Sedulius, but doctus habere occurs at one of the passages cited, 3, 231); cf. also Don. And. 2, 1, 31, and Gell. 6, 17, 3; Ioh. Cassianus, 56, 28; Paul. Pell. 530. doctissimus pan-

---

[1] What does Arch. 4, 161, mean in denying studiosus to Plautus?

dere, S. 2, 93; fingere doctus, S. 2, 645; effingere, P. 11, 129; sollere quaerere, S. 2, 334; solitus descendere, P. 8, 9; nescius: Ps. 143, 883; S. 1, 352; 2, 849; P. 3, 20; but notice nescius above with the gen.; cf. inscius servare, Paul. Pell. 471; inpatiens ferre, H. 133; frenarier, Ps. 191; solvi incapacem, P. 10, 348; (Draeger cites no use of incapax).

5. ABLATIVE.

§61. **Ablative of Manner.** Three usages here may be noted : (a) the abl. of gerund : a characteristic usage of Late Latin is the frequent employment of the ablative of the gerund with a modal force. Often, particularly in Church Latin, it has the force of a present participle agreeing with the subject. Petschenig cites 13 examples of its use in this way in Paul. Petr., and Hatfield comments upon the frequency of its use in Juvencus. In Prudentius, however, its use is restricted: quis hauriendo velit, C. 4, 88; flendo pressit, C. 7, 42; luctando, H. 147; adsciscendo, S. 2, 364; vivendo, S. 2, 660; cf. Priscill. 88, 9; cf. also §82.

(b) With an attribute, common : sese gradu citato proripit, P. 5, 210; praepete cursu venantem, H. 293; gressibus innocuis spatiantur, H. 813; auribus intentis, Ps. 746.

(c) Without an attribute : iure, A. 515; lege, Hpr. 12; fraude, H. 146; ordine, H. 914.

§62. **Ablative of Respect:** fronte severus, Ps. 165; ore severa, modesta gradu, P. 3, 23; fronte serenus, C. 3, 8; fronte vietam, S. 2, 81; pulcerrimus ore, H. 167; mollissima tactu, H. 292; casside terribilis, H. 410; vultu terribilem, H. 947; oculis vaga, Ps. 312 (delibuta comas, in same line); discordes linguis, S. 2, 586; lingua nequior, Apr. (2) 22; tempore senior, numine maior, Apr. (1) 4; arte potens, S. 2, 645; virtute potens, S. 2, 1131; Germine nobilis mortis et indole nobilior, P. 3, 1.

§63. **Ablative of Price,** rare : vendat se spurcis complexibus, H. 634; passeribus venalibus asse, Ps. 620; merce doloris emi, P. 13, 43; hoc milibus emptum, D. 19; campus mercede venditus, D. 153. Cf. also §49.

§64. **Ablative after Comparatives:** sole micantior, C. 5, 44; antiquius caelo, C. 12, 40; licito iactantius, H. 170; plus solito, P. 12, 1; patre deterior, S. 1, 59; quo disertior, S. 2, pr. 56; nive candidius, P. 13, 11; iusto amplius, P. 2, 58; peccante taetrius, P. 2, 285; quo pretiosius, P. 7, 84; purius mysterio, C. 7, 6.

Note. All of the above are in positive sentences, except the last 3, in each of which nil occurs.

§65. Ablative of Degree of Difference: tanto laetior, P. 5, 125; paullo infecundior, S. 2, 955; quanto interius, P. 9, 63.

§66. Ablative of Quality, rare: plenis viribus unum, H. 22; propriis genitum viribus, H. 171; flore perenni virginitas, H. 956; sit stabili fide, S. 2, pr. 38; Ieiunia albo vultu, Ps. 244; ore facundo Cypriane, P. 4, 18; est ulcerosis artubus, P. 2, 153.

§67. Ablative of Means. Prudentius has an interesting example in gradimur fide, S. 2. 907, where the Vulgate has per fidem ambulamus (Ad. Cor. 1, 7); on the other hand, per with acc. is used frequently by Sedulius instead of abl.

(Agent without ab: fratre caesus inpio, P. 5, 171; Juv. also); ablative of means with ab: numen mitigans ab inguine, P. 10, 1067; fames parto fit maior ab auro, H. 257; so also Juvencus, 1, 230; Commod. 65, 8. Fruor, frungor, potior, utor and vescor, together with opus est, are followed by the abl., H. 782; 77; S. 2, 629; P. 10, 105; C. 5, 107; S. 2, 1015; contentus with abl.: contenta decore, H. 264; cf. also A. 184; S. 2, 1128; H. 798.

§68. Ablative after Verbs of Plenty and Want: *Complere* has the abl. 3 times (C. 4, 36, P. 2, 395, 11, 245), the genitive not at all; *inplere* has the abl. 20 times (A. 159, 645; P. 5, 326; S. 2, 944; P. 13, 27, etc.), and genitive not at all; cum is once used: gulam frustis cum inplet, Ps. 424; *carere* with the abl. 12 times (C. 3, 140; A. 267, 671, 894, etc.); *egere*, the abl.: A. 285; S. 2, 232; P. 2, 80; the genitive is not used, though Juv. uses twice, cf. Verg. A. 9, 87; 11, 27; 343; according to Riemann, p. 269, the genitive with egere belongs to the sermo familiaris; *redundare* with abl., A. 717; *abundare*, Epil. 4; eluvie *adfluere*, P. 11, 46; multo *circumfluis* auro, S. 1, 418; *nudare*, Ps. 440; *orbare*, H. 451; *spoliare*, P. 9, 43; *vacare*, H. 781; P. 5, 126; solitis *fraudentur* sumptibus, S. 2, 913; me vel dente vel ungue fraudatum, A. 1068, (but cf. quidquam plenis fraudat ab exequiis, P. 11, 146).

Note. Plenus occurs with the abl.: plenus hoste, P. 1, 100; cf. plenus spiritu sancto, Act. Apostol. 6, 3; plenam Deo, C. 7, 60; P. 2, 542; A. 790; Pspr. 26, (Horace prefers the gen. with plenus). *Egenus* has the gen.: S. 1, 81; 377; 2, 916; A. 423; Ps. 819. *Vacuus*: vacuamque a crimine, A. 899; the usage of Cic., Caes., and Livy. On the other hand Macrob., S. 1, 1, 2, uses vacuus with the genitive of the gerund (cf. also §47). Sine seems to be used in place of ab in C. 10, 34: vacuum sine mente. *Cassus* with abl.: lumine cassis, A. 125; (probably from Verg. Aen. 2, 85, or Stat. Theb. 2, 15); *indigens* with abl.: indigensque victu, C. 4, 54; (Cicero uses the gen., cf. Schmalz', 100). *Abundans* with abl.: abundans luce, S. 2, 887; munere abundans, H. 708, variaque abundans caede, P. 10, 1053. Hier. also uses the abl., but Claud. uses the gen.; cf. IV Cons. Hon. 113.

§69. **Ablative of Place Where.** Such ablatives are common and appear in four forms: •

A. *With an Attribute*, (a) with a preposition, (b) without a prep. B. *Without an attribute*, (c) with a prep., (d) without a prep.

A. (a) *With a preposition:* tristi in arce, H. 111; in cerebro ebrio, Hpr. 57; vitioso in orbe, H. 113; vacuo in orbe, S. 2, 340; eversis in agris, H. 243; beata in regione, H. 954; capta in urbe, S. 2, 694; (b) *without a preposition:* celsa arce, H. 494; nitidis crinibus, H. 272; stabili mente, H. 342; tristi abysso, Ps. 90; ulteriore loco, Ps. 268; latenti chao, S. 1, 94; placito templo, S. 2, 258; culminibus summis, S. 2, 399; digno lectulo, P. 2, 354; terris nostris, P. 4, 114; minutis artubus, C. 12, 113; omnibus aris, S. 1, 129.

B. (c) *With a preposition:* in arce, H. 268; S. 1, 4; in orbe, S. 2, 2; 956; P. 2, 116; in corde, H. 670.

(d) *Without a preposition:* caelo, P. 1, 1; 6, 126; A. 633; rure, P. 3, 38; polo, P. 2, 552; averno, Ps. 92; puteo, H. 833; fine, S. 2, 886; solio, Ps. 875; humo, S. 2, 810; limo, H. 465; P. 10, 371; silvis, S. 2, 875. (Here may be noted: gaudens haerede, Pspr. 49, and fretus amore, H. 495.) Argis, Carris, Delphis (Cretae) occur. It will be noticed that the following combinations occur: tristi in arce, celsa arce, in arce; vacuo in orbe, and in orbe, etc., and that for the most part the prepositions are used or omitted indifferently.

§70. **Ablative of Separation.**

1) *Names of towns:* illud ab sumpsit Athenis, S. 2, 353; fugiens Sodomis, H. 725; but cedere de Sodomis, H. 773.

2) *Common nouns,* after verbs denoting motion: veniunt caelo, C. 10, 77; caelo fluit, A. 370; caelo influebat, C. 7, 75; 9, 6; domo egrediens, S. 1, 215; domo pepulit, S. 1, 530; summo missa throno, Hpr. 10 (Draeger says, only Florus; cf. also caelo vox missa, Juvenc. 1, 163); summo aethere demissus, H. 528; but media ex arce demittunt, H. 312; emissus solio, A. 585; deiectum solio, S. 1, 47; tollunt solo, P. 14, 50; puppi desiliat, Spr. 2, 31; procede sepulcro, A. 742; solitis decedere, S. 2, 312; but a prisco discedere ritu, S. 2, 336; animo depellite, S. 2, 124; subtrahit

indignis, S. 2, 830; cf. Aen. 6, 465, (or dat.? cf. A. 277), but de fomite traxit, H. 115, H. 196; eiecta solo, S. 2, 983; firma statione movebit, H. 501; so Cic. and Caes. with loco, but e muris gressum promoverit, H. 736; and ab omni labe remotis, H. 841; C. 7, 28; caput caligine protulit atra, H. 179; but referens ex hoste, Ps. 64; sede pia procul exigitur, C. 3, 121; foro abriperent virum, P. 10, 816; Roma secesserat, P. 11, 41.

Without a preposition: templo lucis sacratis arcentur, S. 2, 53 (but with ex, S. 1, 414); nos mortis tenebris liberat, C. 12, 164. Pellite corde metum, A. 1080. Mens soluta curis, C. 6, 33; cf. P. 6, 159; H, 911; also after: absolvere, P. 2, 584; abstinere, Ps. 451; deficere, S. 2, 829; emicare, Ps. 325; excerpere, A. 312; excludere, P. 4, 66; exuere, H. 456, 781.

Note 1. Ablative of *Source* or *Origin* is used with: genitus, S. 1, 53, 87; but ex Patre, H. 627; satus, Pspr. 60; patre prosatum perenni, P. 6, 46; nate Deo, A. 418; corde ex natus, C. 9, 10; editus, C. 3, 3; 12, 50; Pspr. 12; S. 2, 824; but (ex) verbo, C. 11, 18; ortus, S. 1, 165; 2, 221; but ex ore, C. 11, 18; manantem Deo originem, C. 5, 30; without either participle or verb: Melchisedech, qua stirpe, quis maioribus ignotus, Pspr. 43.

Note 2. *liber* is followed by abl. without a preposition in: H. 44, 702, 912; S. 1, 144; Pr. 44; C. 7, 24; A. 937; but with ab in P. 10, 519, and C. 5, 135. With the gen. cf. §47.

§71. **Ablative denoting Time When** occurs both with and without an attribute: sero aevo, Ps. 375; tempore longo, S. 2, 344; exitiali die, S. 2, 569: tenebrosa nocte, S. 2, 704: also Ps. 216; S. 2, 917, 977, 1078; A. 628; P. 4, 172; without an attribute: principio, C. 5, 50; H. 155; S. 2, 133; nocte, H. 223; cf. illa nocte, C. 5, 127; nocte dieque, C. 8, 56; H. 514; tempore, A. 825; cf. illo tempore, A. 103; C. 1, 66; annis, A. 350.

Note. Ablative denoting Duration of Time. This occurs frequently after the time of Tacitus and Suetonius, and belongs to the sermo vulgaris; cf. Petronius §111; frequent in Justinus.[1] Occurs not infrequently in Church Latin: Arnob. 2, 25; 4, 26; 15 times in Lucifer Cal., 4 times in Commodian; Paul. Petr. 1, 137; 5, 34; Cyprian (Gall.), centum vixerat annis, Gen. 228; Victor Vit. has duravit in regno annis triginta septem, p. 23. 5; cf. also Eugippius, p. 11, 3; 53, 10; Faustus Rei., p. 134, 12; 286, 10; Ioh. Cassianus, p. 74, 1; Buch Sirach (Latin version) una hora, 12, 14; annis is thus used by Claudianus also, cf. 26–634 (Birt). In Prud.:

---

[1] Paucker, Z. f. ö. G. 1883, p. 326.

Erravit septingentis annis, S. 2, 413; exitiabilis ter denis annis,
S. 2, 715; speculator qui nos diebus omnibus prospicit, C. 2, 105;
Ternis dierum ac noctium processibus mansit, C. 7, 121; secretus
quinis diebus octies, C. 7, 187; tribus cursitat diebus, P. 2, 142;
sex continuis latent diebus, P. 6, 31; tanto tempore tecum versor,
A. 121; (cf. tanto tempore vobiscum sum, Iohan. 14, 9); omnibus
te concelebrent seculis, C. 9, 114; cf. P. 5, 575.

§72. **Ablative Absolute.** This construction occurs in the 4
poems, Ham., Psych., Sym. I and II, 3671 lines, 89 times; 56 times
with the perfect participle, 33 times with the pres. act. participle,
the participles of the deponent verbs not occurring in this construction. In the Cathemerinon, however, the perfect part. out-
numbers the present, as 32 to 6, and one deponent occurs (C. 12,
169).

§73. **Other Ablative Constructions.**
Dignus takes the abl., Hpr. 30; 579; S. 2, 113, 255, 591, 1130;
P. 1, 25; tenendis ossibus, P. 1, 5; indignus also: H. 936; S. 2, 118.
Juvencus also uses the abl., Hieronymus the gen., dignum tantae
feminae, Ep. 77, 8.

Fido and *Confido:* Ps. 26, pectore fidens; fidit iaculis (dat.?),
C. 5, 51; S. 2, 422; Spr. 2, 48; confisa paratu, Ps. 200, but con-
fido sancto in spiritu, P. 10, 104, (this construction first used by
Capitolinus, Draeg.[2] I, 238).

Muto followed by the abl.: corvos mutare columbis, D. 192.

Absque = sine, frequent in sermo familiaris and a characteristic
mark of African latinity,[1] appears very often in Hier., not at all in
Arnob. and Cyprian, here and there in Augustine, (cf. Wölfflin,
Rhein. Mus. 37, 98). It is very frequent in Salvianus, occurs 26
times in Faustus Rei., and 15 times in Cl. Mam. It occurs 3
times in Prud.: nil absque Deo factum, H. 182; absque aliena, A.
43; absque fraude, P. 10, 998; cf. also Vict. Vit. 29, 2; 87, 25.

The ablatives *causa* and *gratia* as quasi-prepositions with the
genitive do not occur.

f) **Participles, Gerund, Gerundive and Supine.**

1. PARTICIPLES.

§74. **Statistical Investigation.** The participle is an important element of style, contributing to condensation of statement,

---

[1] Cf. Kübler, Archiv, 8 (1892). p. 178: "besonders wichtig für Erkenntnis
afrikanischen Sprachgebrauches."

rapidity in narration, and playing an important part in periodic structure. To ascertain what use was made of it by Prudentius and to compare him in this respect with Juvencus and Priscillian,[1] predecessors of the same century and probably of the same country, an investigation was made of the first 500 lines of the Psychomachia, omitting the first 20 lines of introduction, as that poem was less argumentative and contained more narrative than the other hexametrical poems. Complementary infinitives and infinitives after *verba sentiendi et declarandi* were counted as parts of one expression, as : audet spargere, videbat eos fugere. Participial nouns and participial adjectives, as factum, perditus, and ardens, were not reckoned as participles. In these 500 lines there are 495 verb forms to 196 participles (72% : 28%), curiously enough, the exact proportion in Juvencus, though the distribution is different : perfect passive participles 112 to Juvencus' 98; present active participles 74, here again agreeing with Juvencus; gerundive passive participles 1 to Juvencus' 11; future active participles 9 to Juvencus' 3; there should also be noted 2 cases of the ablative of the gerund (lines 84 and 132) which is equivalent to the present participle (§61). If, however, the participial adjectives be included, there are 128 perf. part. to 84 pres. part., making in all 222 participles instead of 196, or 31% to Juvencus' 28%. But some of the lyric poems, especially those in praise of the martyrs, often contain extended passages of narrative, and in these the participles appear in greater numbers, producing rapidity in narrative, one of the features of Prudentius' style in which he appears at his best; P. III and VI may be especially cited. In P. IV, 7–11, there are 6 participles to one verb.

The present participle, to bring out the details of the picture, may be noted in P. 10, 901, also in 902, and in P. 6, 58 ; also in P. 1, 70, where it has the force of a clause with dum ; others might be cited. Notice also the effect of the perfect participle in Ps. 34, 61, 125, 184, 280, 282 in contributing to condensation.

§75. **Present Participle joined to Object after Verbs of Perceiving.** (For which Schmalz[2] only cites Calp. Piso, Cic., Sall., Nepos, Vitruv., Liv. and Horace); Hatfield cites a number of examples in Juv. It occurs but a few times in Prudentius : hunc

---

[1] "Ein Characteristikum der Sprache Priscillians ist der geradezu unmässige Gebrauch von Participien." Schepss. Archiv, 3, 322.

[2] Lat. Synt.[2] §109.

cernet gementem, C. 10, 111 ; fusos rotantem cernimus Tirynthium,
P. 10, 239 ; Laurentium flentem videns, P. 2, 23 ; quosdam videt
offerentes, P. 6, 52 ; quos cantantes stupuit (= saw with amaze-
ment), P. 6, 112 ; cf. C. 5, 30.

§76. **The Deponent in a Passive Sense** is believed not
to occur : for the *perf. part.* in *Middle sense*, see §26.

§77. **Deponent Perf. Part. used Aoristically** : cadavera
animas comitata rapientur, C. 10, 43 ; venerata Deum percenseat
Roma, A. 385; concordia comitata Fidem ridet, Ps. 802 ; filius
arce inlapsus intret, Ps. 819 ; ratus contulit, S. 1, 224 ; diffusus
viribus aptas, S. 2, 31 ; also S. 2, 42 ; P. 2, 447 ; 3, 48 ; 4, 185.

§78. **Future Participle used as Attribute** : paritura, A.
584 ; perituros honores, H. 100; pariturae virginis, H. 575 : mori-
turum (avoided by Cicero, very frequent in Vergil, Landgraf[1])
maritum, H. 586, also H. 914 ; Ps. 583 ; S. 1, 560 ; and others.

Denoting purpose : petit visurus fumum, C. 7, 137 ; petit pugna-
tura Fides, Ps. 22 ; desiluit metatura, Ps. 825 ; it visura, S. 2,
1092 ; veniet positurus, P. 4, 11 ; also A. 684 ; Ps. 473 ; S. 2, 602 ;
cf. petiturus, Apul. Met. 10, 34. For other expressions of purpose
cf. §108, 4, C.

§79. **Present Act. Part. for Perfect**, very rare : infundunt
agmina saturanda crescente cibo, A. 716 ; noctua advolitans pro-
didit, S. 2, 575 ; cf. Paul. Pell. 187, 327, 372, 391, 498; Cypr.
Gall. ex. 196 ; frequent in Eugippius.

§80. **Passive for Active** is believed not to occur ; cf. also §23.

§81. **With Particles** : mox adfuturo deo, C. 7, 52 ; iam rever-
tentem, C. 9, 98 ; iam stantibus, C. 10, 73 ; iam obstanti, H. 212.

2. GERUND.

§82. **In general and in detail** : Prudentius uses the gerund
construction about as often as the gerundive, about 90 of the
former being used to 87 of the latter. With the gerund he uses
but 1 preposition, ad; with the gerundive, 5, ad, de, e, in, and
pro. He uses the gerund about as often relatively as Juv., using
it once in 123 lines to Juv. once in 128 lines. The genitive is
used most often, 49 times, the abl. 36 times, acc. 3 times, and
dat. 2 times, appearing in the following forms :

Genitive, (a) after nouns, as : mos edendi, C. 7, 147 ; amor
habendi, Ps. 478 ; cf. S. 2, 762, 1005, etc.; a noun depending upon
the gen., a very rare usage, occurs : luxus vorandi carnis, P. 10,

---

[1] Landgraf, Archiv, 9 (1894), p. 48.

514 ;[1] (b) after adjectives: fandi nescii, C. 2, 46; expertes furandi,
S. 1, 86; indocilis fandi, S. 1, 647; tacendi intemperans, P. 2,
253; secandi doctus, P. 10, 886; (none of these adjectives exc.
doctus are mentioned by Draeger, §597); cf. also P. 10, 210; C. 7,
161, etc. Note: Gen.=purpose: paenitendi datur diecula, C.
7, 96.[2]

Dative. But 2 cases occur: P. 5, 18, verba mollia suadendo
effuderat ; and A. 15, pietas spernendo libelli tibi est.

Accusative : ad resurgendum, P. 10, 640; ad sacrandum, P. 10,
912 ; ad secandum, P. 10, 1064. It is to be noted that he does
not employ the archaic construction of an object after the gerund.

Ablative. Frequently has a modal force (cf. §61), though it is
often difficult to determine whether it has a modal force or is used
to express means or cause: H. 147; C. 2, 50; 3, 91 ; A. 166; Ps.
84; S. 2, 660; P. 9, 72; 11, 198, etc. Worthy of note: libera
miserando inopum, Ps. 580.

3. GERUNDIVE.[3]

§83. **Gerundive denoting End after Active Verbs**: dedit
sequendam lineam, C. 7, 50; also P. 4, 141; 5, 388; 12, 56; D.
172 ; se praestitit inspicendum, A. 24; P. 10, 601; offerens costas
execandas, P. 10, 73; also C. 4, 45; Hpr. 4; S. 1, 565; 2, 1118;
P. 5, 364; 6, 50; 10, 44, 954 ; 11, 198; D. 58, 154.

§84. **Gerundive with ad, denoting Purpose**: opera ad
divina conrumpenda, H. 179; ad ludibria oppugnanda, Ps. 16; ad
haec colenda, P. 10, 246; efficacior ad devorandas offas, P. 10, 808
(but seminandis efficax erroribus, P. 10, 271); ad decus petendum,
P. 13, 73.

§85. **Gerundive has the force of an Attribute Adjective**: fruenda, C. 3, 84; tremendas, D. 6, 56; tuenda, C. 6, 76;
horrendus, H. 39; Ps. 291; P. 4, 103: 5, 247; 11, 54. Other
forms: C. 7, 37; 45; 83; 133; 9, 75; 85; Apr. 6, 328 ; 453; Ps.
27; H. 260; 735; S. 1, 494; 2, 909; P. 3, 71.

---

[1] For other examples and discussion in general cf. Dosson, De Participii
Gerundivi vi et usu, Paris (1887), p. 86.

[2] Cf. adsentandi in Ter. Ad. 270 and Incert. Auct. ad Her. 1, 16, 29; 2,
30, 48 (Marx).

[3] For general treatment cf. Dosson, as above. Also Weisweiler, Das lat.
part. fut. pass., Paderborn (1890). Cf. also Archiv, 9 (1894), 316 and 317.

§86. **Copula omitted with Gerundive**: dicendum mihi, Pr.
31; vis admiscenda, A. 17; quod vivendum, A. 71; revolandum,
H. 815; idolium fugandum, S. 1, 610; vincenda voluptas, S. 2, 146;
metuenda potestas, S. 2, 171; silendi, P. 4, 181; bibendus, P. 10,
736; but expressed: qui sit dampnandus, H. 128; restituendus
erat, S. 2, 265; subnotanda est, P. 2, 132; mors luenda est, P. 5,
52; mors habenda est, P. 5, 357.

The following *case-usages* may be noted here:

Genitive: indocilis occurs also with gerundive: tractandae
indocilem ratis, Spr. 2, 60 (this adjective is not mentioned by
Draeger); diruendae civitatis incolis, C. 7, 83; consultor habendae
relligionis, A. 453; cf. H. 260, 735, etc.

Dative: chiefly to express purpose or end, and occurs, a)
with nouns, b) adjectives, c) verbs: a) his agendis plectrum, P.
10, 935; b) artibus aptum noscendis, S. 2, 329; also P. 10, 438;
dignus tenendis ossibus, P. 1, 5; (or abl.?), (if dat., not mentioned
by Draeger); neither capax (C. 9, 66) nor efficax (P. 10, 271) is
mentioned by Draeger, §598. c) Descendit servando homini, A.
156; utere sorte blasphemis tenendis, A. 773; cf. also Spr. 1, 67;
P. 11, 151; etc. See §57.

Ablative, with de: S. 2, 407; P. 10, 87; with e: Ps. 259;
with in: S. 1, 458; 2, 820; pro: Ps. 9; S. 2, 919; cf. dignus above.

4. SUPINE.

§87. **Occurrences of Supine.** In -um: probably only;
salutatum, P. 11, 189. In -u: dira relatu, A. 1; visu horridus,
P. 10, 1043; miserabile visu, P. 9, 13; inculta visu, P. 2, 180;
quod dictu scelus est, A. 822.

g) Prepositions.

§88. **Noteworthy Constructions.**
a) post-position: pecudes inter, S. 1, 80; Floras inter, S. 1,
266. This, while occurring frequently among poets, is used with
characteristic frequency by Prudentius, who uses it at least 113
times; cf., besides the above, C. 3, 11; 7, 28; A. 209, 262, etc.
b) Separation of prep. by conjunction: trans et Pyrenas, P. 2,
540. (It is sometimes at quite a distance from its object, as in H.
196, 473; A. 108, 145, 714, etc.) c) *Adusque* occurs in A. 983;
H. 950; Ps. 634; S. 1, 112; P. 10, 364, 560, 763; 11, 190; *usque
ad* also occurs, in local sense, A. 261, 1007; P. 1, 110: in temporal sense, C. 1, 33; S. 2, 280; in genealogical series, Ps. 384;

indicating measure, S. 1, 270; C. 4, 30.[1] Usque ad occurs 11 times in Priscillian, and is very common in Macrobius.

2. Interrogative Sentences.

§89. Interrogative Particle lacking: quaeritis Christicolum genus? P. 3, 72; tu porro solus obteras Caesarem? P. 5, 108; also A. 631, 961, 962; H. 320, 481, 483, 673; Ps. 623, 370; S. 1, 334, 590; P. 2, 316, 320; 10, 410, 445, 946; 11, 4, 256. The above questions are all rhetorical questions.

§90. Si as Interrogative Particle. This is common in eccl. Latin, and two cases have been found in Juvencus, but none in Prud. It was used with a partly conditional, partly interrog. force in Pl. and Ter.,[2] but Prud. seems to have used it only with a cond. force, and never as an interrog. particle, either in simple or complex sentences.

Ind. questions it may be noted are, for the most part, in the subj.: I have noted but one exception: Cernis ut una via est errans? S. 2, 896. This is another mark of his good latinity.[3]

§91. Other Interrogative Particles: *non* = nonne in P. 10, 296; A. 355, 421, 631; P. 3, 112; so also in Commodianus, 2, 33, 10; 32, 7; 1, 14, 6; *ne* = nonne, P. 10, 376, as in archaic Latin; cf. Com. 2, 32, 2; and Lucifer Cal. 153, 1; 201, 4 (Hartel Ed.); *numne* : S. 1, 322; 2, 940; H. 871. (Ritschl. Opusc. 2, 248, denies the Latinity of this form, so also Hand. Turs. 4, 79, but Ribbeck argues for it, Lat. Part. p. 13, and reads it, Afran. fr. 29.) Prudentius' fondness for questions appears in a number of places, but see especially H. 462-490, seven in succession. *Anne* (which gives some support to numne) in a direct question, and before a consonant, S. 1, 400; in an indirect question, P. 10, 963; cf. also Claud. 26, 524; Ioh. Cassianus, 300, 14; *qui* (= quomodo), S. 2, 523: defendere Idam qui hortis potuit?

B. Coordinate Sentences.

§92. Some noticeable cases.

a) *A Series of Imperatives.* These occur both with and without connectives: i, ferrum rape, perfunde cunas, C. 12, 99; conscende rogum, decumbe, P. 2, 354: discede, Iupiter, relinque, P. 2, 453, 465; 11, 30; A. 594; also: conmitte formas et confer, P.

[1] See further uses, Thielmann, Archiv, 6, 469.
[2] Becker, Stud. Stud. 1, 195.
[3] Koffmane, Kirch. lat., p. 130.

2, 221; rape et conice, P. 11, 67; with *nunc:* state nunc, hymnite,
P. 1, 118. (This Schmalz regards, Lat. Synt. §163, An., as the
usage of Vergil, remarking that Vergil does not use et in these
cases, but cf. Aen. 11, 119.) This is the usage of Hor. and Ov.;
Prudentius also uses the connective: nunc suscipe gremioque
concipe, C. 10, 125; and adesto nunc et percipe, P. 5, 545 (cf.
Hor. Ep. 2, 2, 76).

b) *que et* for simple *et:* timorque et ira, P. 10, 962; corpus
pastumque et corporis omnem, A. 722; mentisque et corporis
actu, Ps. 767; aram foresque et ipsas solvere, P. 10, 50; cf. also:
P. 2, 288, 369; 10, 224, 910, 962; (not in Verg. and Hor.,
Schmalz §178). factoque et nomine clarus, Paul. Petr. 3, 267.

c) *ne . . . neve* occurs in S. 1, 78.

d) *et = sed* in P. 3, 2; 240; Vergil uses que for sed, A. 10, 34⁴

C. Subordinate Sentences.

1. Subordination without Relative Pronouns or Particles.

a) Paratactic Constructions.

§93. **Simple Subjunctive**: fugiatis censeo, S. 2, 129, putetis,
131; censeo tollas, S. 1, 425; absolvas precor, P. 7, 79 (reddas
precor, Hor. O. 1, 37); sit supplex precor, C. 8, 77; precor prae-
cipe, C. 10, 165; colas memento, P. 12, 66; moneo fugias, H.
703; deponas velim, S. 1, 499; P. 2, 169; (common in letters of
Cicero, cf. also Hor. O. 3, 16, 38, and S. 1, 5, 53); dicas volo, S.
2, 393; P. 10, 880; opto noverit, P. 10, 441; vis dicam, S. 2, 583;
(but infin.: S. 2, 270; P. 11, 234); faxo teratur, Ps. 249, as frequently in Plautus; reddas necesse est, C. 10, 139; A. 852; P.
10, 169; Quint. 1, 2, 18; (also infin. P. 10, 89, 424); date demam,
S. 2, 732; date perluamus, P. 4, 193; iubet sternerent, P. 5, 260;
praecipit tollant, P. 10, 697. cf. §19.

§94. **Conditional Sentences without Particle**: sit satis,
sufficiat, C. 3, 181; caelum nitescat laetius, gratetur, C. 11, 10;
curramus regumque sequamur progeniem, invenies, A. 997;
respice ad cellam, invenies, S. 1, 573.

§95. **Paratactic Temporal and Causal Construction**:
temporal: vernat herbarum coma, tum laurus obumbrat, C. 8, 45;
emicat columba repens, martyris os visa relinquere, P. 3, 163;
causal: Desine, Christus adest, A. 409; Desine grande loqui,

frangit Deus omne superbum, Ps. 285; also: C. 10, 119; 129; 134; P. 13, 99.

b) Infinitive, and Acc. with Infin.

§96. Final Infinitive. Ecclesiastical writers make free use of the infinitive to express purpose after verbs of motion. Dombart cites 10 examples of it in Commodianus thus used, and 3 times with dare (cf. also Sulpic. Severus, Dial. 2, 6, 6 : venit audire). Prudentius does not use it so freely after verbs of motion, only these two occurring: spoliare viantem adgressus, H. 208 ; ire mandat milites raptare plebem, P. 10, 44. Exceptus admittere, A. 896 ; this is very rare ; the nearest parallel seems to be, natum tolerare labores, Ov. Met. 15, 121. It is most frequent with dare ; I have noticed 12 : dat credere, dat pudere, P. 13, 27 ; dat nosse, C. 6, 44 ; dedit transmittere, Ps. 678 ; also Ps. 644 ; C. 3, 192 ; S. 2, 427 ; P. 2, 336 ; A. 42, etc.; dat ferre, Cypr. Gall., Gen. 1453 ; duat vivere, Commod. 1, 14, 7 ; dedisti posse, Paul. Pell. 569 ; dare with the infin. is used 10 times in Sedulius, in Cyprian 3 times, and in Ennodius 8 times ; cf. datur scire, Comm. ap. 136. Ut also is used: P. 2, 434 ; ne, 13, 67.

§97. Objective Infinitive, after causative and auxiliary verbs : amare, ardere, audere, cavere (but cf. P. 10, 136), certare, cogere, conpellere, contendere, cupere, dedignari, desinere, dignari, discere, exigere, extimescere, emerere (A. 1033) (Draeger says it occurs only 3 times and only in Ovid), gaudere, habere (freq. in Itala and Vulg. Roench. p. 447 ; 11 times in Cyprian), horrere (previously observed only Verg., Liv., and Ammian., says Draeg. §424; but cf. also Cic. Agr. 2, 37, 101 and Lact. 7, 15, 11), instituere, malle, meditari, meminisse (also, memor esse), merere, monere, nescire, niti, nolle, odisse, parare, pavere, pergere (P. 4, 147), poscere, prurire, quaerere, recusare, recipere ("allow," A. 517, not mentioned by Draeg.), sinere, spernere, studere, suadere, subigere, temptare (C. 4, 80, 90 ; 5, 72 ; Ps. 45 ; S. 2, 99, 385, 507, 696 ; P. 10, 877 ; neither Draeger nor Schmalz cites any usages of this after Quint.; I have noticed also the following in Juvenc. 1, 113 ; 2, 476 ; 3, 222, 464 ; 4, 607) ; trepidare, velle, vetare. Note: prohibere is used as in class. period, always with the acc., with the act. infin., as in P. 6, 50 ; C. 3, 169 ; S. 1, 620 ; 2, 463 ; and with the pass., as in S. 2, 1125.

§98. Simple Infinitive as Subject. This is very common and occurs in 3 forms: (a) when the verb is accompanied by a noun, as quis furor est perdere, P. 3, 66; (b) when it is accompanied by an adjective, as facile est frenare, H. 524; and (c) with impersonal verbs, as licet, etc. (a) Tempus (est) cohibere, S. 1, 656; Quae ratio est submittere, A. 642; cernere fas sit, A. 18, cf. also A. 260; S. 1, 351; edere Patris est, Apr. 7; labi hominis, servare Dei est, H. 665; vivere cordi est, Ps. 555; necesse est pensare, H. 615; S. 2, 278; P. 2, 196; (but with subj. P. 10, 134, 210, 990, 1100, and generally cf. above §93). (b) Serum est spernere, C. 1, 10; satis sit dixisse, P. 10, 648; simplex esset credere, Apr. 32; fundere erat melius, H. 98. (c) Licitum est cernere, A. 112; taedet percurrere, H. 273 (Draeger §424, 9, b. says only in Ter. and Ov.); with licet, C. 3, 10; libet, C. 3, 59; piget, H. 376; sufficit, Ps. 458; iuvat, C. 3, 12; H. 420, 471; Ps. 459; P. 3, 137, etc.; with est, Apr. 5; A. 64; P. 11, 131; A. 121; H. 82.

Note. Infinitival clause as subject of a finite verb: dubium est animas de semine Iacob exilium gentile pati, H. 453; quam pudet hoc illis persuasum (esse), S. 1, 283; est perdere tanti vitae officium, H. 652; cf. also P. 10, 672.

§99. **Accusative with Infinitive in Indirect Discourse.** The following verbs may be mentioned as followed by this construction: credere, dederat iudicium tendere se, P. 3, 17; docere, dubitare, ferre, flere, fidere, iubere (also foll. by dat. and inf., and ut with subj., cf. A. 636, 658, 1030, 1069; with simple infin., see P. 10, 40), meminisse, mente tenebo esse, H. 342; ostendere, petere, praedicare, praemonere, prohibere, ridere, suadere (also with ut: H. 718), D. 15.

§100. **Accusative with Infinitive used as Subject:** fuit melius inperium tolerasse patres, H. 463; cuncta creata senescere necesse est, P. 10, 13.

§101. **Other Noticeable Points in use of Infinitive:**

a) Infinitive depends on a verb implied in a noun: indubitata fides, Dominum curare potentem, Ps. 621.

b) Two infinitives: curvare nefas (esse) putantem, C. 4, 41; nosset servare malle, C. 7, 104; miratus (est) posse sustinere, C. 8, 192; Ps. 58; cernere erat splendescere frondes, A. 64; also P. 11, 132; Ps. 395; S. 1, 563; 2, 651; P. 1, 37.

c) Subject, when a pronoun omitted: docuit (me) infectum loqui, Pr. 9; (me) stare iubens, Pr. 21; (eum) spectare mandaram, S. 2, 260; addit (eos) loqui, P. 10, 458; cf. P. 14, 57.

d) With *facere* in the sense of "to cause to": facit imbrem flere, C. 5, 24; P. 13, 45; A. 604, 902; S. 2, 221. This is chiefly colloquial and late, and the usual sense of facere in Ambr., Hier. and St. Aug. (Thielmann, Archiv, 3, 194; but on p. 195 he cites but 2 examples of this usage from Prudentius), Cyprian Gall., Ex. 272: faciunt prorepere ranas; Paul. Petr., Vit. Mart. 2, 76; fecisti evolvere linguas; Commod. Instr. 1, 26, 37: defunctos vivere fecit; cf. also Ap. 117, 122, 619, 624, etc. Caec. Cyprian, Epist. 75, 10: facere se terram moveri; Ioh. Cassianus, 27, 4: cunctos facit consurgere. This use of facere occurs 11 times in Cl. Mar. Victor, cf. also Faust. Rei. 217, 6; Sedul. 3, 335; 4, 18; Claud. Mam. 134, 12; and very frequent in Salvianus.

e) This periphrasis occurs: scio non futurum ut concremur, P. 10, 853.

f) Infinitive in exclamations occurs in P. 10, 803: vos non potesse dissipare!

2. Subordination by Means of Relative Pronouns and Particles.

§102. **A General Relative implying a Condition** not common:

a) quidquid: sufficit quidquid facias, C. 8, 69; quidquid gerimus, spiritus texat, Ps. 767.

b) quisque: quisque deum Christum vult dicere, dicat, A. 1060; also S. 2, 477; P. 5, 784; P. 10, 35; 214: sentiet quisque consecrarit.

§103. **Relative Clauses of Characteristic Result**: nil est dulcius quod iuvare possit, C. 4, 95; quae gens tam stolida quae praeponat, A. 196; possum exempla excerpere quae doceant, A. 313; dignus qui sit, A. 969; indignus qui sancta canam, A. 742; quis erit qui reprehenderit, S. 2, 84; also, C. 4, 30; A. 192, 211; Ps. 516; S. 1, 40, 309, 633; 2, 34; P. 5, 452; 11, 62; 14, 73.

Note 1. Sunt qui with subj. in S. 2, 685; P. 14, 57; with indic., A. 552; S. 2, 841, 865; as also in Commod. C. A. 119. Plautus had used both modes, and both in the same sentence, Curc. 480; Hier. generally uses the indic. (Goelzer, p. 356).

Note 2. Informal Indirect Discourse: Electus Christo locus est, ubi corda probata provehat, P. 8, 1.

§104. **Relative Clauses of Purpose**: nuntius advolare, qui pastum daret, C. 4, 56; facies multiformes fingit, per quas fruatur, C. 6, 39; dextram porrigit cuius sinistra nesciat, C. 7, 218; se praestitit per species quas possit conprendere, A. 25; bis sex adpositi qui bona servarent, A. 740. Further: A. 124, 864; Ps. 915; S. 2, 43; P. 2, 346; 11, 152; D. 17; 134.

§105. **Attraction of Antecedent into Relative Clause**:
non occidet interior qui spirat homo, S. 2, 185; quae pridem con-
diderat iura, vertit, S. 2, 308; quem tu minitaris ignem, flagrabis
ipse, P. 5, 187. Further: Ps. 394; S. 2, 917; C. 6, 79; 10, 33, 41.
Note. Attraction of the case of a relative to that of its antecedent is believed not to occur.

§106. **Other Relative Clauses**:
a) qui = causal: hic locus dignus tenendis ossibus visus Deo,
qui pudicus esset, P. 1, 6.
b) Subj. by attraction: cuius sit fraximus eruta quae conscen-
deret, S. 2, 458.

§107. **Accusative Conjunction.**
1. After *quod.*
a) quod after verba sentiendi et declarandi, very common in
eccl. Latin: occurs 14 times in Cyprian, 11 in Sedulius and 107
times in Hier. (Goelzer, p. 376). Hatfield cites 17 in Juvencus,
but none seem to occur in Prud.; none also with quia and quoniam. This is a mark of his good Latin.
Note. Quod clause as subj. of finite verb seems to occur in:
sit satis quod, etc., C. 3, 181.
b) quod *causal*, with subjunctive to give reason of another as :
increpas ventum furentem quod vertat aequor, C. 9, 37; cf. Ps.
496; S. 1, pr. 31; 2, 38, 912; P. 5, 120; 10, 1048.
2. *Quia.*[1] After verba sent. et decl., 23 times in Cyprian, 16 in
Hier., none in Juv., none in Prud.
Quia *causal*, much less frequent than quod, and followed by the
indic.: quia dedit, haec subdidit, C. 3, 26; moritur quia habet, C.
3, 187; cf. C. 10, 13; H. 25; P. 6, 13. Used interchangeably
with quod, S. 2, 1105; with quoniam, S. 2, 1109. Occurs after
doleas in Ps. 120; doleas quia, the Plautine usage; quia is used
in all 33 times and only once after a verb of emotion (doleo);
miror quod occurs in P. 10, 291, and occurs 3 times in Plaut., cf.
Trin. 290 (Bx); (quia with nam seems to occur but once: S. 1, 53).
3. *Quam* appears with *post* in the form postquam and is followed by the indicative—most frequently by the perfect, then by
the historical present; by the pluperfect in C. 7, 74; Ps. 133; S.
2, 740; by the subjunctive in rident postquam conbiberint Deum,
C. 4, 18; Postquam cadaver retraxerint, procedit inde pontifex,
P. 10, 1042; perf. subj. also in Commod. C. A. 773; appears also

---

[1] I have followed Schmalz (and Lindsay, Lat. Lang. p. 610) in regarding
this as an acc. (Handbuch 2, 501); Stolz regards it as an instr., Id. p. 348).

with *ante*, either joined with it, as in C. 1, 51; or separate from it as in C. 7, 40, and elsewhere; with pres. subj. as in C. 1, 51; imp. in C. 7, 40; and perf. in Pspr. 14, where it follows dedit.

a) Comparative clauses with *quam:* fit peccatum prius, quam inlustret, C. 1, 54; docuit non prius ullum caelestia cernere regna, quam toleraverit, C. 10, 87. (Quod dignius obsequimur quam si recinat, C. 3, 34.) Also: A. 826, 1065; S. 1, 315; 2, 1030; P. 10, 428.

b) quamlibet = quamvis, C. 8, 53; 11, 17; S. 1, 593; P. 11, 163; quamvis with subj.: C. 5, 7; A. 190; 921; H. 226; Ps. 674.

4. *Dum.*

dum, 'while,' with pres. indic.: cardo rotat dum fruimur, Pr. 43, also: C. 6, 25; A. 599; S. 2, 1086; P. 4, 131.

dum 'until,' with accessory idea of purpose, suspense being involved: eo usque dum lux surgeret, C. 2, 75; expectat dum coquat, Apr. 51.

dum joined with adversative signification: dum tumuit vigor, nullus fecundavit amor, S. 2, 1080. (The perf. in both clauses is used by Cicero.)

Note. dum occurs with imp. subj. 4 times in Sedulius, with the pres. once, with the pres. indic. once.

§108. **Locative Conjunction.**

1. *Cum.* The imperf. and pluperf. after cum are regularly in the subjunctive, as, C. 3, 77; 4, 52; A. 234, 308, 1034; P. 11, 6; Ps. 135, etc. I find no case of the imperf. indic. with cum, as in Juv. 3, 98; but with the perf. indic. it occurs in C. 5, 103: cum semel fluxerunt.

2. *Quoniam*, causal, occurs 21 times and always with the indicative: C. 5, 23; A. 516, 1038; H. 694, etc.

quoniam is used by eccl. writers like quia and quod after verba sent. et decl. Cyprian uses it thus 11 times; Hier. but once, Ep. 147, 1 (Goel. p. 384); so also but once by Tert. (Wölff. Archiv, 5, 496; cf. also Arch. 8, 558; 9, 99; 251); Prud. not at all, though he makes use of Ter

3. *Donec*, in the sense of "until" with the subjunctive: permansit donec transvolveventur, C. 11, 30; pugnant donec Christus adsit, Ps. 910; advolevit donec solidaret, S. 2, 331; extendite donec conpago crepet, P. 5, 112; also P. 5, 464; 10, 1040; 12, 36. In the sense of "as long as": pressit donec expavit ignem, C. 7. 44; Juv. used this only in the sense of "until" (H.).

4. *Ut.*

a) *ut*, relative: nec sic tabescunt nives ut seges vanescit, C. 7, 208; sic piratis mare servit, ut mercatori, S. 2, 791; ut dederat palmam, sic tribuit veniam, P. 8, 12; also H. 521; P. 10, 486; 13, 12; 14, 67; Epil. 24.

b) *ut*, temporal: with pres., Ps. 274, 764; with perf.: ut reddidit, tribunal victor adscendit, C. 9. 103; cf. S. 1, 215; P. 5, 365; 7, 36; 10, 1026; with pluperf.: quos ut increpaverat: inpendet, inquit, C. 7, 132; ruit ut (=simul atque) Christum senserat, C. 9, 54.

c) *ut*, final or consecutive, exhibits the usual forms. For other ways of expressing purpose, see §§78, 84, 96.

Note 1. Ut is used with a comparative in: ut pars potentior extet, C. 10, 23; adorat, vuluus ut subiret paratius, P. 14, 86; cf. Priscill. 23, 2. For quo, cf. §110.

Note 2. The negative final clause is always introduced by ne, cf. also ne non, A. 1079; H. 551; ut ne occurs in the consecutive clause: sic haec constare tria ut ne faciam, A. 243.

d) *ut* after verbs of asking, promising, perceiving and teaching: nonne vides ut nulla avium cogitet, Ps. 617; nonne vides ut marceat, A. 479; (cf. also Hor. O. 1, 14, 3, and S. 1, 4, 109); cernis ut vestigia probentur, S. 2, 363; cernis ut una via est errans, S. 2, 896; orant ut celer ignis advolaret, P. 6, 116; qui iubet ut redeam, A. 1069, also 1031; S. 2, pr. 31; memor ut fiam, rogatis, P. 6, 83; rogo ut spectet, H. 308; cf. the paratactic construction §93; (note *ut ne* in: hortante ut ne parcerent, P. 10, 755).

Note : ut introduces a clause explanatory of a noun: populare quiddam credidit frequentia ut autument, P. 10, 81; Dei virtus memorabilis est ut redeat, A. 1058; da hoc ut levent, C. 3, 173.

Note : credis ut incipias occurs in Commod. 1, 34, 19, not 1, 24 19 as given by Dombart (Index).

5. *Ubi* has 3 uses: (a) temporal, where it is construed with the perfect about as often as with the historical present; besides being used with these two tenses, it also occurs with the pluperfect once: ubi regnaverat, texat, Ps. 912; (b) as a relative of purpose: electus Christo locus est ubi provehat, P. 8, 1; consecrat aeterna ubi luce coruscet, Ps. 108; legisse deos ubi sanctior usus maneret, S. 2, 541; (c) as a locative adverb: Ps. 665; S. 1, 573; P. 3, 191; 10, 411; 12, 37; etc.

6. *Si.* On *si* as an interrogative particle, see §90. On conditional clauses introduced by a general relative, see §102.

a) *si* = dummodo: opto inperator noverit, si velit, P. 10, 442.

b) *si* after expressions of the emotions: nec mirum si rotantur, H. 247.

c) *si* in conditions: *a*) Fut. ind. in both clauses, twice: Apr. 11; P. 14, 36; with fut. perf. in protasis, 3 times: C. 10, 142; S. 2, 27; P. 10, 871. *β*) Pres. ind.—fut., 3 times: P. 10, 443; 814; S. 1, 50 (cf. also, quis terror occupat, si expresserit, P. 10, 286). *γ*) with pres. subj. in protasis: *si sit—sit*: 12 in Prud., 3 in Juv.; *si sit—est*: 20 in Prud., 8 in Juv.; *si sit—erit*: 6 in Prud., 10 in Juv. In the relative frequency of usage of these forms Prudentius may be compared with Hieronymus, and Juvencus with Symmachus.[1] *δ*) Imperative in apod. 17 times: Spr. 1, 84; P. 11, 64; 13, 63; etc. With jussive subj. in apod.: Pr. 35; A. 400; S. 2, 14; etc. Cf. further S. 2, 49; Ps. 394; P. 10, 991; C. 11, 94; A. 128, 586; H. 61, 106; etc. *ε*) Unreal conditions, only P. 10, 295; 986; A. 321, (cf. S. 1, 287; 636. P. 5, 402; 11, 81); 9 were noticed in Juvencus.

§109. **Modal Conjunction.** *Quin :* nec nox ulla vacet quin canat, Pr. 38; sic nulla restet mora quin resumat, P. 5, 570. (*Quin corroborative:* this is by far its most frequent use, especially with an added *et*. Prudentius seems to have been especially fond of beginning the line with quin et, using it thus 9 times to Juvencus o times, Hor. 3 times, Vergil 5 times; cf. A. 458; P. 5, 281; etc., immo is added in P. 5, 165, and with potius, A. 294; etiam, in Ps. 851; S. 2, 778).

§110. **Ablative Conjunction with quo = ut.** Quo is thus used both with and without comparatives; without: frequent, referring to a preceding noun, as tu iter monstras quo resurgat, C. 10, 20; 12, 146; H. 250, etc. Also: iugulos opponere quo oppetant, P. 10, 65; but used in this latter way rare. Cf. Commod. 61, 47; 118, 44; 21 times in Lucif. Calar.; cf. Eugippius, 5, 4; 56, 20; Sedul. C. 3, 13; p. 300, 19. With comparatives: superbia volitabat quo se iactantius inferret, Ps. 181; also S. 1, 20; 2, 6; P. 2, 127; with minus, P. 14, 13.

[1] Cf. Blase, Der Konjunktiv des Präsens im Bedingungssatze, Archiv, 9 (1894), p. 25.

D. Characteristic Employment of the Different Parts of Speech.

1. NOUNS.

§111. **Abstracts in -io.** Hieronymus was particularly fond of abstracts in -io and they abound in the Vulgata. They are a mark of the sermo plebeius.[1] Prudentius uses 53, a few not having a clearly abstract signification. None are ἄπ. εἰρ. (marked *), 8 are post-Augustan and late (followed by †), o eccl. The remaining 45 are classical. They occur most often in Ham. and least often in S. I.

List.

In -ion: conditio, conluvio, ditio, legio, oblivio, optio, regio, relligio, (8); cf. also, amasio (†), P. 10, 182, pugio, C. 12, 116 (passage not cited by Fisch, Archiv 5, 82); pusio, C. 11, 13; 12, 104; etc.

In -tion and -sion: actio, agnitio, ambitio, auctio, cognitio, concio, crematio (†), dimensio, discretio (†), divisio, dominatio, generatio (†), habitatio, imitatio, inpressio, indignatio, instauratio, intentio, iussio (†), laceratio, lapidatio, meditatio, natio, obiurgatio, observatio, obstinatio, obstrectatio, operatio, oratio, passio (†), persuasio (†), portio, quaestio, ratio, redemptio, reparatio (†), seditio, simulatio, subiectio, superstitio, supplicatio, transmigratio (†), trepidatio, veneratio, (44). In the use of nouns in -io, Prud. stands in marked contrast to Vergil, 53 : 6. On the other hand, Plautus uses 85[2] and Ter. 22.[3] Three of the 6 of Vergil were employed by Prud.: ratio, seditio, superstitio; 11 were also used by Juvencus.

§112. **Abstracts in -tas and -tudo.** Prudentius uses 64 nouns in -tas and 2 in -tudo. Of these none are ἄπ. εἰρ., 6 are p. A. and late (†), the remaining 58 are classical. Both forms in -tudo are classical, and occur in C. 9; the majority of the forms in -tas occur in the lyric poems. A marked difference from Vergil appears here also: Prud. used 64 to Verg. 19, while on the other hand Plaut. used 72; 14 of those used by Vergil appear in Prud. In -tudo, Prud. used 2, Verg. o, Plaut. 23, Ter. 9. This latter form belongs rather to the sermo vulgaris or to the archaic.

---

[1] Cf. Marx, Auctor ad Herennium Proleg. p. 168.
[2] Rassow, De Plauti Substantivis.
[3] Slaughter, The Substantives of Terence, 1891.

List.

Aetas, aeternitas, antiquitas, anxietas, austeritas, bonitas, caecitas, castitas, civitas, claritas, credulitas, deitas (†), A. 13, 76, 1008; S. 2, 268 (Wölfflin, Arch. 5, 497, does not cite this use), divinitas, duitas, Hpr. 37, edacitas, facultas, feritas, gentilitas, germanitas, inmanitas, inmortalitas, inpietas, integritas, largitas, levitas, libertas, loquacitas, maiestas, malignitas, maturitas, mobilitas, nobilitas, novitas, obscuritas, parcitas (†), pietas, posteritas, potestas, profunditas (†), prosperitas, protervitas, pubertas, qualitas, rusticitas, saevitas (†), sancitas, simplicitas, sobrietas (†), sodalitas, suavitas, trinitas, unitas, urbanitas, vanitas, venustas, veritas, verbositas[1] (†), vetustas, vicinitas, virginitas, voluntas, voluptas. *-tudo:* altitudo, aegritudo.

Paucker, K. Z., 23, 139, does not cite Prud. as using deitas (A. 76, 1008; S. 2, 268); nor parcitas, P. 10, 359; and omits entirely from his list duitas,[2] Hpr. 37.

§113. **Nouns in -men and -mentum.** The forms in -men, being chiefly poetical, we find greatly outnumbering the forms in -mentum. Four words appear in both forms, fig-, frag-, funda-, stra-.[3]

Of the forms in -men, 3 are ἅπ. εἰρ., 1 eccl., 11 p. A. and late, 3 poet. and p. A., 6 occur only in poetry, and 43 are classical.

List of Nouns in -men.

Acumen, agmen, cacumen, cantamen, carmen, certamen, creamen (†), crimen, cruciamen, culmen, discrimen, examen, figmen (†), flamen, flumen, foramen, fragmen, fulmen, fundamen (poet.), germen, gestamen (poet. and p. A.), gramen, hortamen, inritamen (poet.), legumen, levamen, libamen (poet.), libramen (†), ligamen (poet. and p. A.), limen, litamen, luctamen, lumen, medicamen, meditamen (poet.), moderamen, modulamen (†), munimen, nomen, numen, oblectamen (poet.), ostentamen (†), palpamen (†), peccamen (†), perflamen (eccl.), piamen (piaculum also used, cf. §154), purgamen, regimen, *religamen, semen, sinuamen (†), specimen, spectamen[4] (†), * speculamen, spiramen (poet.), *spurcamen, sputamen (†), stramen, subtemen, sufflamen, tegmen, tuta-

---

[1] Taken up also by Gregory of Tours. Cf. p. 196, 16.
[2] He gives it, however, in his list in Beiträge zur lat. Lex. (1872), p. 540.
[3] Prudentius seemed to have been fond of using synonymous expressions. Cf. also §119 and Faguet, p. 90.
[4] Ps. 913, not cited for Prud. by Paucker, Beiträge zur lat. Lex. p. 674.

men (poet. and p. A.), *ululamen, vegetamen (†), velamen (poet. and p. A.), vimen, volumen. (67).

List of Nouns in -mentum.

Alimentum, argumentum, armamenta (H. 560), armentum, augmentum, caementum, calcamentum, cognomentum, deliramentum (Plaut. and p. A.), documentum, elementum, experimentum, figmentum (†), fragmentum, frumentum, fundamentum, incrementum, indumentum (†), lamentum, momentum, monimentum, monumentum,¹opermentum, ornamentum, pigmentum, recrementum (†), sacramentum, sarmenta, segmentum, stramentum, testamentum (31). Of these forms, 3 are p. A. and late, 28 are classical.

Comparing Prud. with Verg., and Plaut. and Terence, notice: in -men, Prud. has 67, Verg. 37, Plaut. 19, Ter. 7 ; in -mentum, Prud. 31, Verg. 14, Plaut. 48, Ter. 14 ; Prud. uses over twice as many forms in -men as in -mentum,.Vergil almost 3 times as many, a usage the reverse of that of Plautus and of Terence.

§114. **Plural of Abstracts**: adfectus, concentus, consortia, contagia, dispendia, divortia, fastidia, gaudia, otia, periuria, pondera, robora, silentia, solatia.

§115. **Plural of Concretes**: cibos, C. 4, 92 ; ciborum, C. 7, 188 ; P. 5, 406 ; colla, Spr. 1, 26 ; P. 10, 750 ; escas, C. 8, 76 ; lucra, C. 2, 44 ; mella, C. 3, 71 ; menta, P. 10, 908 ; musta, S. 2, 218 ; saxi pondera, P. 7, 30 ; tundatur terga, P. 10, 116 ; thalamis, S. 2, 1080 ; aversa vultus, P. 14, 41 ; H. 908.

§116. **Concretes used Collectively in Singular**: miles, Ps. 451 ; S. 2, 518 ; P. 10, 61, etc. (cf. Paul. Pell. 383) ; advena, Ps. 210 ; pusio, C. 12, 104 ; heros, virgo, puer, senex, anulla, P. 6, 149 ; Iudaeus, A. 542. (This usage occurs frequently in Vergil (Ladewig, Ecl. 8, 2.) Here may be mentioned civitas, C. 7, 141.

§117. **Abstract Noun as Subject or Object** occurs frequently, especially in the Psychomachia, where so many abstract qualities are personified. Aetas prima flevit, Praef. 7 ; protervitas et luxus foedavit, Praef. 10 ; pietas extulit, Praef. 20 ; potestas iudicet, C. 4, 97 ; voluntas sapit et captat, C. 10, 25 ; pietas studet, C. 10, 58 ; virginitas et fides bibit, A. 583 ; calor meminit, Ps. 25 ; clementia reprimat, neu sciat invidia, P. 13, 65 ; vim decebat innocenti aetatulae inferre leges, P. 10, 677 ; also H. 424, 627 ; Ps. 248 ; S. 1, pr. 56 ; 2, 504 ; 4, 76 ; P. 10, 1003 ; D. 139, etc. Frequently in Victor Vit.

¹ On these two forms cf. Stolz, Hist. Gram. (1894), I; §172.

§118. **Nouns in -tor, -sor, -trix.** Prudentius uses 149 of these forms: 8 are ἅπ. εἰρ (*), 29 p. Aug. (†), 3 poet., 2 poet. and p. A., 4 eccl., 1 archaic and late; the remaining 102 are classical.

List of Nouns in -tor.

Adsertor, aemulator, amator, animator (†), apparitor, arator, auctor, bellator, cantor, *captator (as used by Pr.), censor, cognitor, conditor, confessor (eccl.), consultor, contemptor, conviciator, creator, cultor, dator, depositor (†), dictator, *dissertator, dissipator, divisor, doctor, dominator, ductor, emancipator (†), exactor, excitator (†), executor (†), extinctor, factor, fautor, fictor, formator (†), fossor, fundator, genitor, gestator (†), gladiator, gubernator, habitator, hortator, ianitor, incohator (†), incitator (†), induperator (archaic and late), infusor, inmolator, inperator, insecutor (†), insidiator, institor, interemptor (†), C. 12, 114, cf. Lucifer, Cag. 53, 6; 148, 25; inventor, *lancinator, largitor, latrator, lector, luctator, mediator (†), mercator, messor, moderator, negator (†), nugator, obsessor, orator, pastor, peccator (†), penetrator (†), percussor, perdomitor (eccl.), peremptor (†), persecutor (†), populator, portitor,[1] praeceptor (†), praestigiator, rector, redemptor, regnator (poet.), repertor, salvator (eccl.), sator, sciscitator (†), scriptor, scortator, sculptor, sectator, sector, secutor (†), servator, signator, spectator, speculator, sponsor, stator, stuprator (†), suasor, successor, sulcator (†), supplicator (eccl.), testator (C. 12, 87; very rare), tortor, traiector (†), triumphator (†), ultor, unctor, unctor, *unicultor, vaticinator, vector (poet. and p. A.), venator, ventilator, *verberator, viator, victor, vocator (†). (120).

In *-trix:* bellatrix, *calcatrix, creatrix (poet., P. 4, 191), dominatrix (A. 88; very rare), donatrix, enuntiatrix, fautrix, genetrix (poet. and p. A.), idolatrix, *inficiatrix, meretrix, moderatrix, negatrix (†), nutrix, obstetrix, ostentatrix (†), peccatrix (†), praenuntiatrix (eccl.), proditrix (†), pugnatrix, redemptrix, saltatrix, speculatrix, spectatrix, *strangulatrix, turbatrix, Ps. 668 (poet. and very rare), venatrix, vexatrix, victrix. (29).

A marked contrast exists between Prud. and Vergil in the use of these forms, but a much more marked one between Prud. and Juv.; in -tor: Prud. has 120, Verg. 50, Juv. 26 (accord. to Hatfield); in -trix: Prud. has 29, Verg. 11, Juv. 1 (H). This seems

---

[1] P. 5, 406; not cited by Paucker, Kl. Beiträge zur Lex. u. Wortb. 1872, p. 481.

to be a marked characteristic of Prudentius, though Tertullian used 150.' Out of the 149 forms in Prud., 108 did not occur in Juv., and 36 of them had been used by Vergil.

§119. **Diminutives.** As diminutives occur in greatest abundance in the sermo familiaris, one could hardly expect to find them in any great numbers in the poems of Prudentius. For purposes of comparison Juvencus and Vergil were also examined. The results are: Prud. employs 55, Juv. 8, Vergil 30; on the other hand, Plaut.² uses 164, Ter.' 34. Of these 55, all are class. except 3 († = post-Aug. and late) ; 15 were previously used by Vergil (V); 4 also by Juvencus (J) ; and 3 of them were used by each of the three poets.

List.

Aetatula, agellus (V J), ancilla, anulla, auricula, bracteola, bucula (V), calculus (V), capillus (V J), chartula, circulus (V), corpusculum, cunulae, diecula, fasciola, fidiculae, filiola, filiolus, flagellum (V), flammeolum, igniculus, lapillus (V), lectulus, libellus, ligula (P. 10, 978), lucellum, muliercula, olusculum, osculum (V), palliolum, palmula (V), papilla (V), particulus, parvulus, paullulum, puella (V J), puellula, pugillus, rivulus, sacellum (V), scalpellum, servulus, sigillum, spiculum (V), stipula (V), tabella, taeniola (†), trulla, ungula († in sense used) (V), vasculum (J), vernula (†) Ps. pr. 22, 57, versiculus, vexillum, virgula, virguncula. (55).

2. ADJECTIVES.

§120. **Adjectives in -alis and -bilis.** The development of these adjectives belongs more particularly to post-classical Latin and is found chiefly in popular Latin. Prudentius shows a fondness for each of these formations, 55 appearing in -alis and 78 in -bilis. Of the forms in -alis, 2 are ἅπ. εἰρ., 8 p. Aug., and 3 eccl.; the total of all the forms in -alis in Prud. is more than twice as many as those used by Vergil, as 55 : 23. Prud. uses 15 forms which had been already used by Verg.

List in -alis : amphitheatralis, armentalis, bestialis (†), *bractealis, bustualis, capitalis, carceralis (†) (also uses carcereus), carnalis (eccl.) (he also uses carneus and carnulentus), coniugalis,

---

¹ Schmidt, -tor et -trix, Ap. Tert., Erlangen, 1878, p. 19.
² Rassow, De Plauti Substantivis, (cf. also Archiv, 9 (1894), p. 313).
³ Slaughter, The Substantives of Terence.

corporalis (†), crinalis, episcopalis, exitialis, fatalis, feralis (poet.
and †), flabralis, fluvialis, furialis, genialis, genitalis, gregalis,
hospitalis, infernalis, inmortalis, intemporalis, iugalis, letalis,
lustralis, maritalis, menstrualis, mortalis, mundialis (eccl.), muralis,
natalis, naturalis, nivalis (niveus and ninguidus also used), noxialis,
oblivialis (†), occidualis (†) (also uses occiduus), palpebralis,
paricidalis, poenalis (†), prodigialis (†), regalis, romphalis, sensu-
alis (†), sepulcralis, socialis, spiritalis (eccl.), *subiugalis, theatralis,
triumphalis, vestalis, vitalis, virginalis. (55).

Of the forms in -*bilis*, 3 are ἁπ. εἰρ., 16 are p. Aug. and late, 5
are eccl., 1 is poetical. While Prud. has used 78 in -bilis, Vergil
used only 27, of which 15 were taken up by Prudentius.

List in -bilis: amabilis, aequiparabilis, *conlaudabilis, conmu-
tabilis, conspicabilis (eccl.), consumabilis (†), contrectabilis (Lucr.
and late), convertibilis (†), cruciabilis, Ps. 446 (rare), debilis,
demutabilis (eccl.), *digladiabilis, dissociabilis, dubitabilis, A. 581
(rare), *excruciabilis, exitiabilis, exorabilis, flabilis (eccl.), flebilis,
flexibilis, formabilis (eccl.), formidabilis, habitabilis, ignobilis,
inaestimabilis, inculpabilis (†), indelibilis, indissolubilis, indoma-
bilis,[1] inennarrabilis, inevitabilis, inexpugnabilis, inexsuperabilis,
inextricabilis, inpassibilis (eccl.), inpenetrabilis, inplacabilis, inpos-
sibilis (†), A. 833, (cf. also Macrob. S. 5, 3, 16; Serv. Verg. Ecl.
3, 107; Don. And. 1, 3, 6, Schol. to Pers. 5, 123),[2] insanabilis,
insatiabilis, insecabilis (Hpr. 61) (†), instabilis, intestabilis, inviola-
bilis (poet. and †), invisibilis (†), invitiabilis †), liquabilis (†),
lacrimabilis, medicabilis, memorabilis, mensurabilis (†), mirabilis,
miserabilis, mobilis, mutabilis, nobilis, passibilis (†), placabilis,
probabilis, propitiabilis, penetrabilis, perflabilis, praenobilis (†),
remeabilis (†), resolubilis, revocabilis, solubilis, stabilis, sufflabilis (†), terribilis, tolerabilis, vegetabilis (†), venerabilis, veniabilis (†), violabilis, visibilis (†), vitiabilis, volubilis. (78).

§121. **Adjectives (and Participles) as Substantives.**
This usage appearing already in the pre-classical period, occurs
with greater frequency in the classical period, being advanced
by Sallust and the Augustan poets, but finds its greatest development in late Latin. Prudentius, as Juvencus before him, makes
free use of this method of expression. A complete catalogue
cannot be given here, but the following may be noted:

[1] Per. 5, 11; not cited by Paucker, Kl. Beiträge zur lat. Lex. u. Wortbild.,
1872, p. 473, nor p. 641, nor in Materialen zur lat. Wortgsch., p. 67.
[2] For its use in the Vulgate, cf. Am. Journ. Phil. 15 (1894), p. 351.

a) *Substantive-Adjectives modified by Attributive Adjectives:*
dissona texta, C. 10, 6; clara insignia, C. 12, 65; senex fidelis,
Pspr. 1; pessimi principes, Pspr. 38; arcana incondita, P. 5, 840;
pia sacra, Ps. 848; sacra mortua, S. 2, 761; secretum grande, S.
2, 843; mortales inopes, S. 2, 916; triste sacrum, S. 2, 1116;
aspera praecepta, P. 9, 25; tristia visa, P. 9, 25; triste longum, P.
14, 107; semetra *dissona, Ps. 829; tenerum decorum, Ps. 826;
grande profundum, S. 2, 90; nivale profundum, P. 12, 38;
secunda bona, Ps. 727. Prud. makes free use of the nom. and
acc. plur. neut. as Vergil did before him (Verg. Aen. 7, 562,
Ladewig); praesens utile, P. 10, 541.

b) *Masculine and Feminine Adjectives used substantively:*
Hier., according to Goelzer, used such freely, 88 examples being
cited. Prudentius does not show so many examples, but 12 in
the singular and 7 in plural, exactly the converse of Quintilian,
who uses many more in the plural than in the sing.[1]

List. Aeternus, ferox, inustus, Iudaeus, iustus, parvulus, pro-
fanus, proximus, rusticus, sacratus, sapiens, supplex; fessi, fideles,
fortes, muti, perfidi, superi; and *participles* much more freely, the
plural prevailing, as: balans, precans; adcubantes, adstantes, audi-
entes, bellantes, circumstantes, comitantes, credentes, discrepantes,
distantes, inruentes, languentes, morientes, obsequentes, peccantes,
pereuntes, precantes, revetentes, scrutantes, sepulti, supplicantes,
tuentes, viventes, vocitantes. Substantivized adjectives are very
frequent in church Latin.[2]

c) *Neuter Singular:* aequum, altum, arcanum, bonum, castum,
grande, honestum, inane, inmensum, iniustum, iussum, iustum,
meritum, mirabile, mirum, nubilum, peccatum, populare, probatum, profundum, sacrum, serenum, solidum, sublime, superbum,
utile, verum.

d) *Neuter Plural* (omitting common participial nouns, such as
facta, errata): abdita, acerba, ardua, aspera, aucta, bona, caelestia,
calcata, candida, celsa, condita, confusa, contraria, cuncta, declivia,
devia, divina, ethica, examina, extima, falsa, fluentia, fragosa,
frivola, furta, futura, ima, inania, inconcessa, inepta, inflata, intel-
lecta, magna, minima, mira, mortalia, multa, mundana, nobiliora,
occulta, omnia, orsa, parta, parva, penetralia, peritura, physica,
prona, prospera, proxima, redacta, sacra, sancta, scelerata, secreta,

---

[1] Cf. Hirt, Archiv, 7, 303.
[2] Cf. Koffmane, Gesch. d. Kirchenlateins, p. 53.

suavia, summa, superna, terebrosa, terrea, terrena, terrestria, tur-
bida, vanissima, ventura, vera, vitalia, viva.

Note. On the appositional and partitive genitive after these
forms see §§41, 45.

§122. **Freer Use of Comparative.** But few such occur:
inridet Asclepiades laetior, P. 10, 921 ; sedebat celsior in solio, P.
11, 50; age ipse maior carnifex, P. 5, 148; laetior ait, P. 14, 68 ;
altius reposta, P. 13, 51.

§123. **Comparison by Aid of Adverbs.** Prudentius sometimes forms the comparative by using an adverb, in which case he
always uses magis, the particle used in Spanish Latin,[1] and never
plus. Claudianus, Bell. Poll. 126, uses magis insignis. Sidonius
and St. Augustine, on the other hand, inclined to plus. Occurrences: magis saporum, C. 4, 94; magis debilem, P. 2, 235;
mage cruda, P. 13, 19; mage potens, P. 3, 10; magis utile, H.
710. Cf. also in Claud. M. Victor. 2, 157; Ioh. Cassianus, 174,
20; Paul. Pell. 411. Cf. Verg. Aen. 4, 31 ; 5, 725 ; Hor. S. 1, 3,
142, and 2, 4, 13; Quint. 10, 1, 94.

Note 1. Prud. does not use magis with the comparative, a
usage of Plautus and of some of the late writers, and especially of
African latinity.[2] Paul. Pell. uses magis with comp. 10 times and
Cl. M. Victor. uses it thus 3 times. Cf. Commod. C. A. 478,
magis plenius; but, plus levior, C. A. 5; cf. Vict. Vit. 24, 14:
magis laudabilior ; Sedul. 246, 18: magis amplius.[3]

Note 2. Longe with the comparative (cf. Schmalz, Stilistik,
§11) : longe diffusius, S. 1, 316; and longe efficacior, P. 10, 807 ;
so, longe tranquillior, Juvenc. 3, 605; longe periculosius, Claud.
Mam. 23, 1.

Note 3. Compounds with prae- also occur, as, praenobilis, prae-
liber, praecalidus, praedives, praedulcis, praepollens, praesiccus.

§124. **Adjective for Adverb.** Besides the classical usage of
adjectives expressive of emotion, others also occur : sumas laetus
libensque carpas, C. 4, 67 ; conscendunt celeres, C. 5, 55 ; faciles
rapi, volentes subeunt, H. 429; si mendosus agit quid, A. 975 ;
altior insurgens, Ps. 31 ; tuta resistit, Ps. 144; saevus inussit, S.
2, 671 ; laetus revertit, P. 1, 14 ; diversa permovet, P. 2, 387 ;
haec ludibundus dixerat, P. 2, 409 ; vise libens, P. 13, 62 ; dimitte
libens, H. 937 ; cf. libens fateor, Faust. Rei. 167, 11 ; cf. §128.

---

[1] Sittl., lokal. Versch. d. lat. Spr., p. 175.
[2] Cf. Wölfflin, Lat. u. rom. Komp., p. 72, and Sittl, as above, p. 117.
[3] For further examples cf. Paucker, Rhein. Mus. 35, p. 606.

51

3. Pronouns (and Adjective Pronouns).

§125. **Pronoun Omitted.** This occurs sometimes with participles, sometimes with the infinitive. For the latter, see §101, C.

§126. **Suus + quisque**: adsignare deos proprios sua cuique iura, H. 105; omnibus posita est sua cuique arula, S. 1, 236; sua quemque cogit velle potestas, C. 8, 67; suum quibusque reddito, P. 2, 94.

§127. **Interchange of Pronouns.**

a) nullus for nemo: H. 534; S. 2, 1126; C. 10, 119; P. 5, 158; cf. Plaut. Merc. 35; Rud. 369; Cl. Mar. Vict. 3, 250; 19 times in Priscillian; Ioh. Cassianus, 11, 10; Eugipp. 29, 9; 38, 20. A frequent usage in Script. Hist. August.[1]

b) nemo for nullus: nemo opifex, A. 519; neminem diem, P. 10, 744. This usage belongs to the popular language. Cicero uses nemo with words descriptive of persons.

c) ullus = aliquis: quae corporis ullo sinu se tegat, Ps. 741.

d) totus = omnis: totum hominem, Ps. 217; totus miles, Ps. 450; P. 9, 11. This is especially frequent in Apul. Met.;[2] frequent also in Commodianus and Sedulius; cf. Paul. Petr. 1, 271; 2, 18; Ennod. 14, 26; 76, 13.

e) ullus occurs after ne in S. 1, 178 and S. 2, 449; aliquis after ne: H. 946; cf. Lucif. Cal. 22, 6; Cl. Mam. 51, 8.

f) quisque = quisquis. Frequent:[3] C. 7, 216; A. 22, 1060; H. 867; Ps. 784; S. 2, 497; P. 10, 35; 129; 214; so also in Commod. A. 611, 749, 803; Paul. Petr. 1, 315; 6, 67; and once in Ammian. Marcel.;[4] Min. Fel. 13, 1; Priscill. 7, 25; Cypr. Gall. Ind. 237; Claud. Mam. 158, 15; 189, 4; Cl. Mar. Vict. 1, 198; and Sid. Ep. 5, 17; Oros. 285, 1; Vict. Vit. 3, 19.

g) quis = qui, frequent: quis furor, Ps. 351; quis vultus, P. 5, 129; quis sensus, P. 5, 421; quis error, P. 10, 404; quis stupor, P. 10, 581; quis deus, P. 10, 999, etc., and in African inscriptions, as 1027, 2729.

h) alius quisquam: H. 183.

4. Adverbs.

§128. **Neuter of Adjective in place of Adverb**: pravum, C. 4, 98; triste, C. 5, 50; suave, C. 5, 122; aeternum, C. 12, 17;

[1] Paucker, Subrelict. Lex. Lat., p. 68.
[2] Wölfflin, Rhein. Mus. 37, 108.
[3] Neue, Formenlehre, 2³, p. 469, cites only H. 867.
[4] Petschenig, Archiv, 6, 268.

grande, Ps. 285; lene, H. 797; indomitum, Ps. 295; formidabile,
Ps. 295; sublime, P. 10, 697; iustum, P. 1, 15; probatum, P. 10, 366;
sanctum, P. 10, 366; fidele, P. 10, 428; iuge, P. 4, 143; iners, C. 6,
36; malignum, P. 5, 417; mortale, A. 37; sanum, P. 10, 247;
inpune, C. 12, 136; longum, P. 10, 393; dulce, P. 10, 365; molle,
P. 10, 281; and others. See also §124.

Note. *Mage*[1] occurs 4 times and only before consonants: S. 1,
517; 2, 6; P. 3, 9; 13. 19. It occurs 14 times in Paul. Petr., 3
times in Cl. M. Victor., Ennod. C. 1, 9, 119; Cypr. Gall. In. 192;
Claud. Mam. 204, 7.

§129. **Adverbs in -im.** These occur much more frequently
in Prud. than in Juv., as 30:7 (the latter number being all Huemer
cites in his index to Juv.). Livy showed a marked preference for
these forms. Of Prudentius' list, 25 do not appear in Juv. The
complete list for Prudentius is as follows, those marked (J) being
also in Juvencus, those marked (‡) not cited for Prud. by Funck
in his list in Archiv, 8, p. 98 ff: adfatim (‡), articulatim, carp-
tim (‡), congregatim, cumulatim, cursim, digestim, frustatim (Ps.
720, omitted on p. 500, ‡), furtim (J‡), gradatim (‡), guttatim,
iunctim, membratim (‡), minuatim (‡), mixtim, particulatim (‡),
passim (J‡), paullatim (††‡), permixtim, raptim (J‡), scissim, se-
gregatim, sensim (‡), sparsim, statim (‡), summatim (‡), undatim,
vicatim (‡ omitted entirely, cf. p. 505), vicissim (J‡), viritim (‡).

5. NUMERALS.

§130. **Use of Composite Form.** These appear, a) with distributives as: mense bis quino, P. 10, 78 (ter quinis, Cypr. Gall.
Gen. 202); sex septena nomina, A. 943; septem septenis, A. 992;
quinis diebus octies, C. 7, 187. b) With cardinals: bis sex
adpositi, A. 739; bis septem, D. 21; tris quater, P. 3, 12; ter
quinque, D. 93; cf. also P. 4, 1; C. 7, 38; P. 4, 53; 173; Ps. 839; S.
2, 423; 462; 715; 1060.

§131. **Distributives for Cardinals.** A number of instances
occur, as: septenos decies in ortus, A. 1004; ternis processibus,
C. 7, 121; cf. trina decennia, Paul. Pell. 232; discipulis duodenis,
Ps. 850; duodeni fasces, S. 2, 424; centena milia, Ps. 481; notice
P. 4, 49: tribus aut duobus forsan et quinis aliquae placebunt; ter
senos, Pspr. 22.

---

[1] Donatus, ad Ad. 2, 3, 11, says: mage pro magis ἀρχαισμῷ.

6. Particles.

§132. **Use of Negative Particles.** Prudentius uses *non* relatively to *haud* much more frequently than Juvencus, as 248 is to 20 in the former, to 61 to 17 in the latter. He differs from Juvencus further in not using haud mora at all ; in not using haud veni or haud poterat : in using haud but twice with aliter (S. 1, 638 ; 2, 831), with which he also uses non as in P. 3, 56. He uses haud with the verbs nocet and placet; with dubium est twice ; and it occurs most frequently with some form of dubius, or dubito. He also uses it with adjectives, as haud sterilem, S. 1, 258. Furthermore there is a striking difference between the number of occurrences of haud in Prudentius, 20, and the number used by Vergil, 120 (Kennedy, Verg. p. 637).

Note 1. Non unquam occurs in: H. 165; S. 2, 115; 1061; P. 5, 433; 10, 295. Haud unquam : A. 10.

Note 2. *Nec non et* occurs in H. 222, Ps. 559, S. 1, 50; P. 1, 10; 5, 485; 14, 5; 10, 1024; C. 4, 5; in all, 8 times. I have observed this 15 times in Vergil,[1] cf. also : Juv. 10, 51 ; Clandianus, Rapt. Pros. 1, 266 ; Com. 2, 18, 6 ; 19, 13 ; 24, 14 ; and in prose : Cypr. 238, 14 (H.); Eugippius, 1, 12; 4, 9; Vict. Vit. 7, 13; Ennodius, 354, 3 ; later, Gregory of Tours, p. 344, 23 (B.). See further, Krebs, Antib. II[a], p. 123.

§133. **Other Particles.**

a) *Ast* (archaic) is used by Prud. 19 times, while Verg. used it 16 times (Horace did not use it in his lyric poems or in his epistles[2]) ; it always occurs before vowels ; Prud. uses *at* 34 times to Vergil's 168 times. Ast occurs much oftener, relatively to at, in Prud. than in Verg.; ast before adjectives, Ps. 649; S. 1, 93; ast ubi, P. 3, 26, appearing also in Verg. and Juv.

b) *exin* (archaic) occurs 6 times, twice in the second place (C. 7, 126 ; P. 2, 161) ; Verg. uses it 4 times and always in first place (Wotke).

c) *Particles of Comparison:* haud secus ac si, H. 804; S. 2, 60 ; haud aliter quam si, S. 1, 638 ; non aliter quam cum, H. 208.

d) *ob* occurs in C. 3, 184; H. 321; S. 1, 444; 2, 489; P. 10, 76 ; 197 ; 13, 88 ; *propter* but 2 times : Ps. 858 ; S. 1, 419.

---

[1] Kübler. Archiv, 8 (1892), p. 181, cites only 8 examples ; to his list add Geo. 2, 452 ; 3, 72 ; Aen. 3, 352 ; 4, 39 ; 5, 100 ; 6, 595 ; 8, 345 ; and read Aen. 1, 748 for 788 in his list.

[2] Cf. Luc. Mueller, De Re Metr.[2] (1894), p. 501.

e) *ab* occurs 90 times, and always before vowels; Augustine, on the other hand, used it 9 times before consonants (cf. Archiv, 3, 149); abs is not used.

7. VERBS.

§134. **Frequentatives.** Almost all of the frequentatives used by Prudentius are classical, 62 out of 63, and 19 are also in Juvencus.[1] One is *ἅπ. εἰρ.* (*), 1 is poetical, 1 poetical and p. Aug.

Frequentatives in Prudentius : advento, advolito (used but once, S. 2, 575), agito, apto, canto, capto, certo, cesso, cito, *concrepito, P. 11, 56; coniecto, crepito, cursito, despecto, dicto, disserto (dubito),[2] exagito, excito, expecto, exsulto, fluito, gesto, habito, iacto, incanto, incito, inperito, inserto, insulto, involito, lapso, latito, minitor, moto, nato, obiecto, occulto, ostento, palpito, pavito, penso, pervolito (poet.), pulso, quasso, rapto, recepto, respecto, resulto, (poet. and p. A.), retento, sector, specto, subiecto, suppedito, suspecto, sustento, territo, tracto, vecto, vendito, verso, victito, vocito, volito.

III.—PROSODICAL AND METRICAL.

1. IN GENERAL; THE HEXAMETER.

The general rules of versification are, for the most part, adhered to very closely. Violations of prosody occur, chiefly in the direction of quantities, but not with such frequency as in the verses of some of the writers of his own age, or of the age immediately preceding him. Much careful work has been done in this field by Krenkel.[3]

§135. **Hiatus** is admitted much less frequently than by Vergil himself, and that too in a century characterized by a somewhat lax treatment of hiatus (cf. Teuffel, Rom. Lit. §403. 2).

These cases may be cited :

1) radice Iesse editus, C. 12, 50.
2) aram ante ipsam simplices, C. 12, 131.
3) hunc posteri Efrem colunt, C. 12, 189.
4) vade homo adflatu nostri praenobilis oris, H. 698.

---

[1] Compare Hatfield's list, p. 34.

[2] Dubito : not regarded as a freq. by Georges and Stowasser ; but cf. Lindsay, Latin Language, 1894, p. 482.

[3] Krenkel, De Aurelii Prudentii Clementis Re Metrica (1884).

5) Tene, o vexatrix hominum, potuisse resumptis, Ps. 58 (or Teneō | vexa | etc. ?)

6) dum tribuit, nosmet dona ad caelestia vexit, Ps. 86.

7) induerat thoraca humeris squamosaque ferri, Ps. 126.

8) occupat interitu: neque est violentius ullum, Ps. 494.

9) praeceptor Belia mihi, domo et plaga mundus, Ps. 714.

10) muneris auctorem ipso de munere pendas, S. 2, 109.

11) spemque in me omnem statuat nunquam peritura, S. 2, 159.

12) unus ego elementa rogo, nec mole laboris, S. 2, 227.

13) immo ita est, armis et viribus indiga veri, S. 2, 510.

14) pulsam utrimque et ad ossa secat, P. 3, 134.

15) ni illa vis exercita, P. 5, 133.

16) spes si qua tibi est, si quid intus aestuas, P. 9, 96.

17) cui est origo caelum, C. 6, 34.

18) his membra pergunt urere ut igniverint, P. 10, 1078. Cf. also H. 287; P. 10, 832; 925, and Luc. Müller, Re Metr.' p. 330 and p. 171.

The unelided vowels of Nos. 3, 10, 11, 12, 17, 18 are in the arsis (ictus syllable); 1, 2, 4, 5, 6, 8, 13, 14, 15 and 16 in the thesis; 1 and 3 are before proper names, 10 before a caesura, in all of which hiatus is permissible (Luc. Müller, Re Metr.' p. 375). There are 7 occurrences of hiatus in Juv., both Hatfield (p. 35) and Huemer (Index) omitting 1, 126.

§136. **Elision** is much less frequent than in Vergil, and somewhat more frequent than in Juvencus. According to Hatfield there are 232 cases of elision in the first 500 verses of the Aeneid and 105 cases in Juv. 1, 1–500. Prudentius, on the other hand, has 150 in the first 500 verses of the Psychomachia, largely based on Vergil; elision occurs most frequently in the 2nd and 4th feet, 44 in the 2nd, 41 in the 4th; in 5th foot, 10 cases occur.

Note 1. Elision after the 6th arsis (aphaeresis): I have noted 38 of these in the hexameter poems, and 28 in the four bks. of Juv.: Huemer cites 11 instances in Sedulius, but has wrong reference in one of them (1, 321).

Note 2. Eskuche, R. M. 45 (1890), p. 417, gives the number of cases of elision of the 3rd form (after the dactyl of the 5th ft.) in Prud. as 1 in 858 lines, instead of 1 in 1029 lines. Prud. has 5 of this form, Juv. 0; Prud. has about 4 times as many cases of elision after the 5th trochee, over 3 times as many after the 5th arsis, as Juv.

§137. **Special Cases of Shortened Syllables.**
Final o is frequently short, both in verbs and nouns. Krenkel gives a list of 51 verbs in final ŏ and of 52 nouns in ŏ. A few omissions occur in his lists of occurrences: cogŏ, H. 702; exigŏ, H. 702; latrŏ, S. 2, 791; meditatiŏ, H. 91; nemŏ, P. 10, 237; virgŏ, S. 2, 969 (but virgō, S. 2, 1090); Junŏ, S. 2, 497; also in adverbs: ergŏ, S. 2, 882; porrŏ, H. 22, 147; postremŏ, P. 10, 968. Also duŏ frequently, H. 4, 11, 21, 68, etc.: notice duŏ, H. 11, and 2 lines below duō; H. 350 contains duŏ twice; ergŏ, S. 2, 204; 220; 750. Of ŏ in the ablative sing. of the gerund, Krenkel cites 18 examples; Huemer (Index) cites 7 examples in Juv.
Cui appears 7 times as cŭĭ (A. 173; P. 4, 4, etc.); once as cŭĭ, S. 2, 114; once as cuĭ, C. 3, 167 (Cl. Mar. Vict. 1, 457, cŭĭ; 2, 158, and 3, 320, cŭĭ; cf. Orient. Carm. 3, 3, cūī; Ennod. 130, 15, cŭĭ) ; and frequently as a monosyllable. Martial also used it as a dissyll. Cf. further Luc. Müller, De Re Metr.² p. 318.

§138. **Treatment of Genitive Forms in -ius** : illīus occurs 3 times, A. 534; S. 2, 669; P. 1, 85; this is the Horatian usage, illīus occurring only in S. 1, 10, 57. Occurs also in Paul. Petr. 4, 367 ; and ipsīus, 3, 285.

§139. **Spondaic Verses.** 29, possibly 30, such verses occur : A. 266, 285, 817, 864, 932, 1038; H. 76, 103, 144. 222, 266, 390, 422, 622, 713, 722, 859 ; Ps. 98, 594 ; S. 1, 43; 111 ; 189 ; 468 ; 603; 2, 267 ; 364 ; 566 ; 856 ; 919 ; and possibly H. 450, which ends with deflens Ieremias ; but more probably, dactylic. (A dactyl occurs in every case in the fourth foot except in H. 450.) But three such verses occurred in Juv.

§140. **Characteristics of Prudentius' Verse, and Table.** The verse of Prudentius is noticeable for its lightness, in direct contrast to that of Juvencus, which was remarkable for its heaviness. In this respect Prudentius comes next to Val. Flaccus and Ovid, the first two in lightness of verse of the 15 poets selected by Drobisch (Ein statistischer Versuch über die Formen des lateinischen Hexameters), his verse being about 5 per cent. heavier than that of Ovid and over 10 per cent. lighter than that of Juvencus and about 5 per cent. lighter than that of Vergil (45 per cent.) Prudentius' proportion is :

d : s :: 50.66 : 49.34, that is, the dactyls and spondees are almost evenly balanced.

Like Vergil and Juvencus, he indicates the character of the verse by beginning more often with a dactyl than with a spondee.

He has in the first foot 62.29 per cent. of dactyls to 37.71 per cent. of spondees. He thus begins with a dactylic movement almost 3 per cent. more frequently than Vergil, and about 7 per cent. more frequently than Juvencus. Considering the movement of the verse as a whole, it may be noticed: 1) the frequent repetition of the same movement in a following line, as ddss Ps. 424, 5; ddds Ps. 383, 4; 485, 6; dddd S. 1, 370, 1; etc., or 3 lines of same movement, as dsds 343f; ddss Ps. 356f; or 4 lines, as, S. 2, 776f; H. 703f; he has 5 groups of these 3-line movements, 278f, 529f, 572f, 917f, 956f.

2) For variety a converse movement in the following line is very frequent, as dddd in S. 2, 815, and ssss in 816; dsss in one line, sssd in foll. in H. 87, 125, 177, 262; S. 1, 526; or dsss and sddd in Ps. 182, 273.

3) In the first 436 lines of Ham. ssss does not occur, and up to the 603 line only twice, 437, 457. But considering in detail the metrical composition of every verse of his four great hexametrical poems, we find the dactyls and spondees arranged in the following schemes :

TABLE.

Book.	SSSS	SSSD	SSDD	SSDS	SDSS	SDSD	SDDS	SDDD
Ham.	9	13	23	44	101	34	72	40
Psych.	19	20	22	68	103	46	37	30
Sym. I	19	8	17	33	52	43	60	24
Sym. II	18	20	33	72	107	68	91	37
Totals	65	61	95	217	363	191	260	131
Per cent.	1.77	1.66	2.59	5.91	9.89	5.20	7.08	3.57

Book.	DDDD	DDDS	DDSS	DDSD	DSDD	DSDS	DSSD	DSSS
Ham.	39	84	102	77	52	121	70	83
Psych.	41	73	115	56	52	90	51	92
Sym. I	21	54	64	40	42	81	50	49
Sym. II	45	86	112	68	71	142	76	86
Totals	146	297	393	241	217	434	247	310
Per cent.	3.98	8.09	10.71	6.57	5.91	11.83	6.73	8.45

Total of verses examined, 3668

Notice : a) ssss, with a high average in Juv., 9.78, has the remarkably low average of 1.77 ; in the Aen. it $=7.20$;[1] Ovid and Claudian alone of the 15 poets have averages lower than this, and the lowest average of any one book of the Aeneid is 5.4 (Bk. 10).

b) The scheme dsds reaches an average of 11.83, while that of Juvencus was 9.25. But 5 books of the Aeneid have higher average than this (III, IX, X, XI and XII), while the lowest average is 9.16 (Bk. V). The average of the 15 poets is that of Prudentius, 11.8.

c) Another contrast between the two poets comes out in the fact that, while dddd is the lowest scheme in Juvencus, ssss is within $\frac{1}{10}$ of being the lowest in Prudentius.

d) Comparison of the four favorite schemes :

	Prud.	Per Cent.	Juv.	Per Cent.	Verg.	Per Cent.	15 Poets.	Per Cent.
1st	DSDS	11.83	DSSS	16.08	DSSS	14.29	DSSS	15.
2nd	DDSS	10.71	DDSS	12.40	DDSS	11.71	DSDS	11.8
3rd......	SDSS	9.89	SDSS	10.87	DSDS	11.05	DDSS	11.
4th......	DSSS	8.45	SSSS	9 78	SDSS	9.58	SDSS	10.

Notes. (1) The favorite scheme of Prudentius is dsds, the 5th in order with Juvencus, the 2nd with the 15 poets.

2) ddss is the 2nd in order both with Prud., Juv., and Verg., and is the 3rd with the 15 poets.

3) The 2nd and 3rd forms of Prud. are the same as the 2nd and 3rd of Juv.

4) The four favorite schemes of Prud. are the same as the four favorite schemes of Verg. and of the 15 poets, but the fourth scheme of Juv. is 15th with Prud.

§141. **Accent in its Relation to the Ictus.** In the third and fourth centuries accent began more and more to assert its claims, and the number of verses constructed according to accent, not quantity, more and more to increase.[2] In the fourth century minute attention was given by the grammarians to the differences between the quantitative verse and the accented verse. Mar. Victorinus (G. L. 6, 206) asks: "rythmus quid est?" And in the

[1] From statistics made by the Latin Seminary of Johns Hopkins University, 1887.

[2] Cf. Stolz, Hist. Gram. d. Lat. Spr. (1894), I, §38, 2.

preceding century, Commodianus, a writer of whom Prudentius made some use, wrote hexameters in which the word-accent counts for more than the metrical value of the syllables. In order to ascertain what influence accent had upon the verse-structure of Prudentius, the first 500 lines of the Psychomachia were examined, and the conflicts of word-accent and verse-accent noted. A similar number of lines were also examined from Juv., Bk. I, and from Vergil, Aen. I. *The results are:*

1) Verses with no conflict of accent, i. e. verses which can be read with regard to accent merely:[1] Prud. has 2, Juv. has 1, and Vergil has 6.

2) Verses with but one conflict: Prud. has 50, Juv. has 49 and Vergil 82. But in a large proportion of the cases this one conflict is in the 3rd foot, due to the occurrence of the caesura. This ought hardly then be counted; (Prud. has 48 verses with the one conflict at this foot, Juv. has 40, and Vergil has 59); accordingly Prud. would have 50, Juv. 41, and Verg. 65 verses with no conflict of accent.

A marked difference is seen between Prud. and Vergil, and that is, that Prud. has but 2 verses in which the conflict is not in the 3rd foot, while Vergil has 23 such verses; Juv. too has but 9, and therefore as many verses with no conflict as verses with one.

§142. **Table showing number of Coincidences of Ictus and Accent,** also showing number of feet composed of one or two words:

	I.		II.		III.		IV.		V.		VI.		Totals.
	Har.	Wds.	Har.	Wds.	Har.	Wds.	Har.	Wds.	Har.	Wds.	Har.	Wds.	Harmony.
Prud.	391	162	204	2	90	1	270	46	498	184	499	280	1952 or 65 07 %.
Juv...	358	175	152	1	47	2	188	32	497	168	500	277	1742 or 58.07 %.
Verg.	363	143	201	2	124	1	188	23	496	179	496	285	1868 or 62.27 %.

{ Har. = coincidence of ictus and accent.
{ Wds. = feet consisting of 1 or 2 words.

[1] In this investigation secondary accent (Stolz, Hist. Gram. I, §89) is taken into consideration, and it should be remembered that all statements refer to the entire verse, and not merely to the first 4 feet.

Notes. (1) Prudentius gives slightly more attention to accent than does Vergil, and considerably more than does Juvencus.

(2) Prudentius' verse exhibits many more instances of harmony of ictus and accent, both in the opening measures and in the close, than does either Juvencus or Vergil, and the difference is very striking in the 4th foot, there being over 80 more cases of harmony there than in the same foot in the verse of either Juv. or Verg., which practically amounts to saying that there are over 80 verses more in Prudentius with the close of the verse capable of being scanned merely with regard to the accent.

(3) The larger number of instances of harmony in the 4th foot in Prud. is very largely caused by that foot being so frequently composed of a word or 2 words; this occurs over twice as often as in Verg. and 14 times more than in Juv. This involves also the relative frequency of the occurrence of the bucolic diaeresis.

(4) With these three poets the 2nd and 3rd feet each are very rarely composed of 1 or 2 words, but 5 in the 2nd foot, 4 in the 3rd.

(5) The verses of Prud. and of Juv. run along with less smoothness, and the lines have less of unity and energy, than the verses of Vergil, there being fewer caesurae in them than in those of Vergil.

(6) In Juvencus, 1, 352, occurs a verse with diaeresis at each foot: nunc sine, nam decet hoc, sic sancta per omnia nobis; this is very rare.

(7) Noteworthy: Prud. Ps. 135 f. has 3 lines with but one conflict of accent; 150 f. has five such lines in succession.

2. OTHER METRES.

§143. **The Iambic Trimeter.** In Prudentius the rythmical flow again approaches the canons of the Greek trimeter. A large per cent of the odd feet are spondees, notably in the 5th foot. Most of the feet are thus iambi or spondees; the other varieties are sparingly used. In all 1519 iambic trimeters occur, of which 1360 are grouped in strophes of 5 verses each; 28 occur in couplets alternating with the dimeter; the remainder, 131, occur κατὰ στίχον.

In these 1519 trimeters:

(1) The *dactyl* occurs only in P. 10; in the 1st foot 6 times, 31, 651, 788, 791, 841, 1004; in the 2nd foot 0 times (cf. 301, 968); in the 3rd foot 8 times, 259, 644, 669, 896, 948, 952, 963, 981; in the 4th foot 0 times; in the 5th foot once, 667.

(2) The *anapest* occurs 96 times in 1st foot (89 in P. 10, 7 in C. 7); in 2nd, 3rd and 4th feet 0 times; in 5th, 41 (38[1] being in P. 10); in Horace only 5 times.

(3) The *tribrach* occurs in 1st foot once, P. 10, 675; 2nd foot 11 times, Apr. 39; P. 10, 301 (ignoscŏ), 333, 703, 753, 758, 771, 784, 876, 968 (postremŏ), 1101; in 3rd, 4 times, P. 10, 587, 764, 856, 978; in the 4th, 13 times, P. 10, 109, 193, 237 (nemŏ), 346, 416, 481, 550, 592, 641, 713, 767, 837, 978; in 5th, 0 times.

(4) *Proceleusmaticus* does not occur.

(5) But one *pure iambic* line was noted, P. 10, 156.

Note. Notice P. 10, 788, amator is the reading of the Mss. Wbmq; animator pronounced anmator? Cf. Romance derivatives.

(6) **Close of Verse.** Noteworthy are:

(1) Contrary to usage of Plautus (Luchs) he has a final iambus preceded by a Cretic word: P. 10, 71; 155; 292; by a word ending in a Cretic: P. 10, 706.

(2) Two iambic words at end, 12 occur: C. 7, 46; 171; 195; Hpr. 1, 7, 23, 60; P. 10, 452; 484; 499; 780; 943. Also with elision in the 5th foot, P. 10, 736; 854.

(3) With 3 iambi at end: P. 10, 175; 498; 706; 802; 938; 957; 963.

(4) With monosyllable at end, 6: C. 7, 59; Pspr. 59; P. 10, 506; 927; 1006; 1119, all parts of the verb esse.

(5) Other forms: Cretic word, 94 times; 4 syllables, 73; 5 syllables, 21; 6 syllables, 2. P. 10, 109 ends with ∪∪∪ | ∪ — | ∪⌣.

§144. **Sapphic Metre.** Prudentius has written 280 verses in this metre. A comparison was made between his usage and that of Horace in an equal number of verses (C. Sec.; Bk. IV, 2, 6, 11 and III, 27 (1–64). The following are the results:

a) *Caesura:* difference in usage quite marked: Prud. has the penthemimeral in every case, Horace has the trochaic 52 times.

b) *Elision* at the caesura: Prud. has 1 (P. 4, 62); Hor. 3 (3, 27, 10; 39; C. S. 26).

c) *Elision* between 3rd verse and adonic: Prud. has 0; Hor. has 2 (4, 2, 23; C. S. 47), -que each time.

d) *Hiatus* before the adonic: Prud. 1 (P. 4, 27) -um; Hor. none.

e) *Hiatus* between the other verses: Bet. 1st and 2nd, Prud.= 10, Hor. = 1; bet. 2nd and 3rd, Prud. =4, Hor. = 1. Prud. has hiatus after -um 5 times, ă 3 times, ĕ 2 times, o 2 times, i 1 time, and ae 1 time ; Hor. after -em, and after -um.

f) *Elision* between the other verses: Prud. o; Horace 1 (4, 2, 22) -que, between 2nd and 3rd.

g) *Elision* within the verse (omitting aphaeresis).

	1st ft.	2nd.	3rd.	4th.	5th.	Adonic.	Total.
Prud.	2	3	1	2	2	0	11
Hor.	1	3	3	5	4	0	17

Note.—Luc. Mueller, Re Metr.², p. 357 does not cite P. 4, 125.

h) *Spondee* in 2nd foot. Both Prud. and Horace have this.

i) *Vocalic ending* of verse (Quint. 9, 4, 93). Difference quite marked : Prud., vowel long = 89, short 121 ; Hor., vowel long = 128, short 82.

j) *Monosyllabic ending :* Prud. has 2, but each is preceded by a monosyllable ; Hor. has 4, but 2 are preceded by a monosyllable, 2 by a dissyllable. Horace has in all only three cases of this last kind. (Luc. Mueller, Re Metr.², p. 263.)

k) Forms of the *adonic.* This clausula appears in Prud. and in Hor. together in 8 different forms : (1) munere donat : Prud. 24, Hor. 41 times ; (2) lege coerces : Prud. 28, Hor. 18 times ; (3) pallor in ore : Prud. 3, Hor. 5 times ; (4) in mea vota : Prud. 4, Hor. 4 times ; (5) quos veneramur : Prud. 2, Hor. 1 time ; (6) fons et honoris : Prud. 1, Hor. o time ; (7) est hederae vis : Prud. o, Hor. 1 time ; (8) Christicolarum : Prud. 8, Hor. 1 time ; (cf. Prud. C. *8, 80 ;* P. 4, 76 ; *80 ;* 112 ; *152 ; 156 ;* 188 ; 192 ; of these, 4 are proper names.)

l) *Two strophes connected :* Prud. connects strophes without a full pause in the sense, 6 times ; Horace 6 times as often, 36.

It will be noticed then in the above that Prudentius differs most widely from Horace in his treatment of the caesura ; in allowing hiatus between the Sapphic verses ; in following almost exactly the reverse of Horace's practice in his treatment of the close of the verse, in employing elision less freely within the Sapphic verses and using aphaeresis 3 times in the adonic, that his 2 favorite forms of clausula are the same as those of Horace, though Horace uses Form 1 almost twice as often as Prud., and that he differs from him quite markedly in using one word only in this foot.

§145. **Alcaicus Hendecasyllabus.** This occurs only κατὰ στίχον, P. XIV, 133 lines. An equal number of verses in Horace were also examined (Bk. IV, Carm. 4, 9, 14, 15 ; III, 29, 1–27).

Prudentius follows Horace closely in introducing the verse with a long syllable, in using a spondee invariably in the 2nd foot, and in using a caesura after the second foot. The first foot, it may be noted, is always a trochee (but cf. 27, 69, 81, 124). The following variations, however, may be noted:

a) *Elision.*

	1st.	2nd.	3rd.	4th.	5th.	At the caesura.	Total.
Prud.	18	0	4	4	0	aphaer. = 4	26
Hor.	6	0	5	0	2	" = 2	13

Prud. elides i 3 times, Hor. elides it 0 times; 0, 3 times to Hor. once; Prud. also elides ae once and u twice.

b) *Hiatus* between the verses. Here the difference is quite marked, though of course only the first two lines of the strophe could be examined in Horace. 11 cases occur in Prud., 0 in Hor.; after ae twice, a 4 times, um 2 times, 0, i, and u, each once.

c) *Caesura:* Prudentius invariably after the 2nd foot; Horace shows 3, (3, 29, 17; 4, 9, 21; 4, 14, 17).

d) *Monosyllable at end*, or before caesura. Of the former, 1 case in Prud. (24); of the latter, 1 case in Horace (4, 4, 73).

e) *End of verse.* Here there is quite a difference: while in Horace the final syllable is about as often long as short (68 : 65), in Prud. the short syllables are more than twice as often used as the long (91 : 42).

IV.—ALLITERATION.

§146. **Classes of alliteration.** One of the marked characteristics of Prudentius' style is his fondness for alliteration. Whether it was because he liked the effect thereby produced, or because he thought that this would make it more clear just what words were to be grouped together, or both, at any rate we find it frequently existing between noun and adjective, especially when separated some distance from each other. Other constructions are thus joined together, as noun and dependent genitive, verb and ablative of means, but it is most frequent between adjective and noun. Alliteration assumes a prominent part in other Christian writers, as in Commodianus, Paulinus Pell. and Cl. M. Victor; so also in Ausonius; Kantecki (p. 80) had treated this subject, though he omits some of the most remarkable examples. Krenkel (p. 46) adds to his lists the occurrences of this figure at the end of the verse. But the occurrences are much more

frequent than one would judge from their lists, and it is believed
that the examples given below added to the lists of Krenkel and
Kantecki will show how frequent is this figure in Prudentius.
Employing Wölfflin's classification,[1] I find that alliteration appears
in the following forms:

a) *Between two nouns:* pelagique polique, H. 192; nebu-
lique et nube, A. 1014; flatibus vel fidibus, C. 3, 82; vultuque et
voci, Ps. 196 (cf. visuque et voce, Juv. 2, 605); ferroque flam-
maque, Ps. 754; generi gentique, S. 1, 35; ruris reditu et ratione,
S. 2, 1005. But 2 occurrences in Juv. (H.).

b) *Between two adjectives:* laxus et liber, C. 8, 65; exul et
errans, C. 10, 168.

c) *Between two verbs:* rapiuntque ruuntque, H. 237 (cf. Aen. 4,
581); canunt calcant et, C. 5, 124; fundavit et fixit, C. 12, 179;
conpremit et cogit, A. 142; condidit et coegit, H. 117; piget,
pudescit, paenitet, C. 2, 26, cf. Praef. 11; dissipat ac donat, Ps.
603, vulnerat et vibrat, Ps. 696; mansuescit et mitigat, mergam,
P. 5, 435; also, P. 10, 580; 1038; 11, 136; 12, 59.

1. **Alliteration between words having some gram-
matical connection.**

a) *Between noun and adjective,* very common: gelida gran-
dine, C. 5, 98; plena paena, P. 4, 135; lunarique lampade, C. 5, 6;
fons fluens, C. 4, 10; vipereis venenis, P. 13, 57; foedere falso,
H. 426; also, H. 690, 759; P. 6, 156; C. 3, 148; 5, 8; 42; etc.

b) *Between a verb and its object:* flecte faciem, C. 3, 7; curvare caput, C. 4, 41; tribuit tribunal, C. 6, 98; setasque sumit,
C. 7, 152; saecula sensit, S. 2, 641; cineresque consecravit, P. 13,
98; etc.

c) *Between a verb and its subject:* non natus nuntiat, A. 591,
mens maneret, C. 1, 59; facies fingit, C. 6, 38; pietas probaret,
H. 627; caper caeditur, S. 1, 129; fuligo fuscat, P. 10, 1117; etc.

d) *Between a verb and modifying adverb:* dulce delectat
Deum, P. 10, 365; cursant congregatim, P. 7, 143; perpessi
plerumque, S. 2, 957; secat salubriter, P. 10, 502; formidabile
fervet, Ps. 296; sanum sapis, P. 10, 24 (cf. sane sapis, Plaut. Amph.
449), etc.

2. **A recurrence of similar sounds:** suffundere fumo, Ps.
45; arce cerebri, H. 312 (cacophony); placabilis inplet, Ps. 636;
ore et pectore, P. 5, 562; amore et ore, P. 13, 3; fluit ac diluit, P.
8, 5, etc.

[1] Die Allitterierenden Verbindungen d. lat. Spr., Munich, 1881.

3. **Alliteration between three or more words**: conum
caesus capita et sinuamine subter subductus conchae in speciem,
Ps. 871, 2; supplicare stipiti, verris cruore, scripta saxa spargere,
P. 10, 381, 2; fraude floret fertile fecunda fundens, Hpr. 53, 4.
Kantecki omits a number of such occurrences as, tunc tibi non
terris tantum, S. 2, 65; milia multa prius peragit quam plaga
pandat polum, P. 3, 62, 3; revertenti reparata in membra redibit,
A. 1073; paucosque non piorum patitur perire, C. 6, 95; also C.
7, 80; 128; 146; 216; 9, 60; 10, 169; 12, 42; A. 706; H. 720; Ps.
280, 549; S. 1, 454 (4 v's); S. 1, 490; 2, 224; 637; 888; 951;
1005; P. 3, 116 (6 f's); P. 4, 123; 147; 6, 140; 10, 540; 1011; P.
11, 76; and others.

V.—ASYNDETON.

§147. **Classes of Asyndeton.** Another characteristic feature
of Prudentius' style appears in his fondness for asyndeton, not
only in groups of two or three words, but also in whole verses and
series of verses. In H. 545, Ps. 448, 464, 2 such verses occur; in
H. 395, 3 verses, and in P. 10, 328, 7 verses occur, all without
connective particles. He uses in all 46 such verses, of these 9 are
in the hexameter poems. Juvencus and Vergil were examined to
see if any such asyndetic verses occurred in them. They seem to
have avoided using such entirely. Horace, it was found, had but
2 (A. P. 121, and Ep. 2, 2, 180). The following classes may be
cited:

a). COPULATIVE ASYNDETON.

I. **Single Words**.
(1) *Asyndeton enumerativum.* a) With nouns: C. 1, 42; 93;
94; 2, 39; 40; 3, 12; 18; 198; 199; H. 395, 396, 397, 761; Pspr.
30, 31, 448, 449, 464, 465; P. 5, 328; 6, 149; 10, 627; P. 14, 106;
H. 349, 358. b) With verbs: C. 1, 87; 2, 26; 4, 82; 83; A. 804;
P. 5, 131; 10, 508; 509; P. 13, 101. c) With adjectives: H.
545, 546; P. 3, 210; 5, 72; 80; 159; 259; 467; P. 6, 35; 10, 33;
347; 1128; epil. 2.
II. **Clauses**. a) Imperatives, see §92, a. b) Other cases:
horrent facies, ambitio ǀtumet, doctrina superbit, personat elo-
quium, fraus nectit, H. 398, 9; vegetat praecordia, frigida suc-
cendat, riget arida, dura relaxet, S. 2, 383; also C. 9, 28; Ps. 493;
S. 1, 256; 2, 389; and many others.

b) EXPLICATIVE ASYNDETON.

Very common: quae ceu dormientes egimus: vigilemus, hic
est veritas, C. 1, 93; laudate omnes inbecilli ac mortui: iam nemo
posthac mortuus, C. 12, 205; non desunt exempla meae virtutis
in ipsis seminibus: natura docet revirescere cuncta post obi-
tum, S. 2, 195; also P. 10, 509; Ps. 553; and others. See also
§§ 94, 95.

c) ASYNDETON SUMMATIVUM.

With *omnes:* Iudaea, Roma et Graecia, Aegypte, Thrax,
Persa, Sycha rex omnes possidet, C. 12, 202; Omnia, chlamys
atque corona, virga potestatis, cornu crucis, altar olivum, Ditt.
79; Romanus, Dalia, Sarmata, Vandalus, Hunnus, Gaetulus,
Garamaus, Alemannus, Saxo, Galaulas, una omnes, S. 2, 808;
also: C. 1, 93; so also, Paul. Petr. 2, 400; involvit omnia, tigna,
aras, statuas, caementa, saxa, metallum.

VI.—PRUDENTIUS AS AN IMITATOR.

§148. **Vergil and Horace the Chief Models.** Both Vergil and Horace were largely utilized, Vergil the model for the
dogmatic and controversial poems, Horace for the lyric.[1] In the
case of Vergil, reminiscences occur from every book of the Aeneid,
from every book of the Georgics and from a few of the Eclogues.[2]
Of the Aeneid, Bks. II, VI, and VIII seem to be most often
drawn upon, IX, X and XI least often; but the 2nd Bk. of the
Georgics has been drawn upon as much as all the rest of the
books of the Georgics put together. In some of these cases there
can be but little doubt that Prud. had Vergil before his eyes when
he wrote; in others it is no less certain that the imitation was either
indirect, through the medium of some preceding writer, or unconscious and not felt as such, to such an extent did the phraseology
of Vergil permeate much of the literature of the post-Augustan
age, both sacred and profane; in some cases also the phrase is to
be regarded simply as parallelism in expression. Prudentius
differs from Juvencus in the greater frequency with which he

---

[1] In the Cathemerinon, Ambrose also has been largely followed. Cf.
Boissier, La Fin du Pag. 2, 112 ; 142.

[2] The Appendix of Ribbeck's Vergil, Ed. Mai, cites only 6 parallel passages in Prudentius.

quotes either whole verses or parts of verses. Juv. never quotes a
verse entire, and half verses but rarely ; Prud., on the other hand,
quotes a verse and a part of another twice, as S. 2, 498, a quota-
tion of Aen. 1, 17 from dea to fovetque ; and S. 2, 53, of Aen. 7,
778 from etiam to equi. A number of the half verses also reap-
pear, but in this, as in all comparisons of the two poets, it must be
borne in mind that the corpus of Prudentius contains over 3 times
as many verses as that of Juvencus.

§149. **Simple Imitation—Vergil.**[1] The use that Prudentius
has made of Vergil appears more particularly at the beginning or
end of a verse.

a) *At the beginning of a verse*, Prudentius uses the Vergilian
phrase, haec ubi dicta dedit (Aen. 8, 541, etc.; Cyprian Gall.
Iesu N. 749; see also Petron. Sat. §61, and earlier, Lucilius, Fr.
17 (Baehrens), on this introductory phrase) once, Ps. 823 : Juv.,
however, according to Hatfield, used it 6 times, and in a slightly
modified form 4 times more. Haut mora, occurring in Juv., does
not occur ; so also the phrases, illi inter sese, and iamque dies ; ast
ubi, only in P. 3, 26; sic ait, only in Ps. 121, and haec ait, only in
A. 147. Principio is used but once, H. 338 (Juv. once, Verg. 10
times, Hat.). Other phrases may be noted, as, dixit et, Ps. 305
(Aen. 1, 402), Quin et, S. 1, 554 (Geo. 2, 30 ; Aen. 6, 777), also A.
458, etc.; non aliter quam, H. 208 (Geo. 1, 201), haud secus, S. 2,
610 (Aen. 8, 414), and H. 804. Of other verses beginning with
the same words, notice :

Possum multa sacris exempla excerpere libris,
Ni refugis, A. 312.
Possum multa tibi veterum praecepta referre,
Ni refugis, Geo. 1, 176.
Sed quid ego haec autem, A. 741, Aen, 2, 101 ; but this occurs
in Sil. VI, 110, and probably goes back to Enn. Ann. 210.
tantus amor terrae, tanta est dilectio nostri, A. 1027,
tantus amor terrae neu ferro laede retunso, Geo. 2, 301 ; here
the recurrence of the metrical scheme dsss increases the resem-
blance.
per loca senta situ, P. 3, 47, and Aen. 6, 462.
nonne vides ut, Ps. 617 ; A. 479, and Geo. 3, 250 (so also Hor.
Od. 1, 14, 3 ; Sat. 2, 5, 43).
fare age quem videat, A. 129 and *fare age* quid venias, Aen. 6,
389.

[1] Treated in a general way by Zaniol, Aur. Prud. Clemente, Venice, 1890.

mane salutatum, P. 11, 189, and Geo. 2, 462.
cui tantum de te licuit, A. 769, and Aen. 6, 502. ּ
felix qui indultis *potuit*, H. 330.
felix qui potuit, Geo. 2, 490, and Juv. 1, 92.
at domus interior, Ps. 868, and Aen. 1, 637.
et dubitamus adhuc, S. 1, 587, and Aen. 6, 806.
Vulcani martisque dolos, S. 1, 626, and Geo. 4, 345. ּ
sed iam tempus, Geo. 2, 542, and S. 1, 656.
Talia vociferans, Ps. 253, and Aen. 2, 679. Cf. also, A. 485,
and Ecl. 3, 103 (Juvenal, 1, 130). A. 64, P. 11, 131, and Aen. 6,
596; 8, 676; C. 14, 105, and Geo. 2, 464; S. 2, 661, and Aen. 8,
579; Ps. 31, and Aen. 12, 902; A. 112, and Aen. 10, 344; Ps. 517,
and Geo. 3, 480; P. 14, 105, and Geo. 2, 464.

At the end of the verse:
virtutum populus *casu concussus acerbo*, Ps. 798;
at pater Aeneas *casu concussus acerbo*, A. 5, 700.
orbe novo *nulli subigebant arva coloni*, S. 2, 282;
ante Iovem *nulli subigebant arva coloni*, G. 1, 125.
—*cuneis scindebant fissile lignum*, S. 2, 285, and G. 1, 144.
—*caesis custodibus arcis*, S. 2, 545.
—*caesis* summae *custodibus arcis*, Aen. 2, 166.
—*aut pelle Libystidis ursae*, S. 2, 300, and Aen. 5, 37; 8, 368.
inproba mors *quid non mortalia pectora cogis?* H. 149.
vi potitur, *quid non mortalia pectora cogis?* Aen. 3, 56.
Here the same metrical movement occurs in both, dssd. Cf.
also Gregory of Tours, h. F. 6, 36, p. 276, 15; and p. 339, 26;
—*si credere dignum est*, Ps. 497, and Geo. 3, 391.
—*dumque oscula dulcia figo*, A. 599;
—*atque oscula dulcia figet*, Aen. 1, 687.
—*ramis felicibus arbos*, A. 338, and Geo. 2, 81.
—*spumantia cymbia lacte*, A. 472, and Aen. 3, 66. Cf. also: Ps.
685, and Aen. 8, 703; A. 662, and Aen. 1, 80; Ps. 879, and Aen.
12, 208; D. 140, and Aen. 3, 659; S. 2, 281, and Geo. 2, 22; H.
278, and Aen. 4, 532, 564, 819; S. 1, 125, and Aen. 4, 215; S. 1,
353, and Aen. 11, 481; S. 2, 331, and Aen. 2, 639; S. 1, 361, and
Aen. 6, 572; S. 1, 94, and Aen. 2, 61; Spr. 2, 13, and Aen. 1, 87;
A. 459, and Aen. 6, 254; S. 2, 532, and Aen. 8, 698; H. 237, and
Aen. 4, 581; S. 1, 523, and Aen. 4, 636; H. 776, and Ecl. 2, 65;
Ps. 786, and Geo. 3, 533.

Both at the beginning and at the end:
nimborum dominum *tempestatumque potentem*, A. 662;

*nimborum*que facis *tempestatumque potentem*, Aen. 1, 80.
Christe, *graves* hominum *semper miserate labores*, Ps. 1 ;
Phoebe, *gravis* Troiae *semper miserate labores*, Aen. 656.
sinum lactis et haec votorum liba *quotannis*, S. 1, 113;
sinum lactis et haec te liba Priape *quotannis*, Ecl. 7, 33.
—*Baccho caper omnibus aris*
caeditur et virides, S. 1, 129;
—*Baccho caper omnibus aris*
caeditur et veteres, Geo. 2, 380, with similar metr. structure.

-que joined to the two closing words :

Prud.	has 12 in	4950	hexameters	=.025	per cent.		
Juv.	" 13 "	3210	"	=.041	"		
Verg.	" 54 "	12912	"	=.042	"		
Ennius[1]"	8 "	426	"	=.188	"		

From which it will be seen Prud. uses this ending, relatively,
the least frequently, Juv. and Verg. about the same number of
times, while Ennius uses it relatively over 4 times as often as
Verg. or Juv., and over 7 times as often as Prud.

b) *Similar phrases are taken into other parts of the verse :*
et regnare simul *caeloque ereboque* putatur, S. 1, 360;
voce vocans Hecaten *caeloque ereboque* potentem, Aen. 6, 247.
omne revolamus *sua per vestigia* seclum, S. 2, 279;
atque in se *sua per vestigia* volvitur annus, Geo. 2, 402.
omnipotens dederat *studia in contraria* vertunt, H. 307 ;
scinditur incertum *studia in contraria* volgus, Aen. 2, 39.
Conrupta *de matre nothi* Ledeia proles, S. 1, 228 ;
supposita *de matre nothos* furata creavit, Aen. 7, 283 ;
Thebana *de matre nothun*, Aen. 9, 697.
et ne iacta *viae* spargantur *in aggere* graua, S. 2, 1032;
Qualis saepe *viae* deprensus *in aggere* serpens, Aen. 5, 273,
with the same movement, sdsd.

Cf. also : H. 498, and Geo. 1, 349; Ps. 394, and Aen. 2, 142; P.
2, 529, and Aen. 1, 94.

An interesting passage occurs in S. 1, 126: atque avidus vini
multo *se proluit* haustu, and spumantem pateram at pleno *se proluit* auro, Aen. 1, 739. Verg. used impiger, Prud. uses avidus
vini ; Verg. used spumantem pateram, Prud. paterae spumis;
Verg. hausit, Prud. haustu ; Verg. auro, Prud. gemmantis.

[1] Fragmenta Poet. Rom. (Baehrens).

In the lyric measures may be noted:

et *ad astra* doloribus *itur*, C. 10, 92 ;

sic *itur ad astra*, Aen. 9, 638.

socius *calor ossa* revisat, C. 10, 38 ;

calor ossa reliquit, Aen. 9, 475.

per *amoena vireta* iubet, C. 3, 101 ;

—et *amoena virecta*, Aen. 6, 638.

furiarum maxima, Ps. 96, and Aen. 3, 252. Cf. also, C. 9, 12 ; and Geo. 4, 392.

§150. **More Indirect Imitation.** Here are included those phrases of Vergil which have been more or less changed, such as :

aves sub ipso culmine, C. 1, 13 ;

volucrum sub culmine cantus, Aen. 8, 456.

pectus sepultum crimine, C. 1, 35 ;

somnosque vino sepultam, Aen. 2, 265.

multo et se fasce levarat, Ps. 578 ;

ego hoc te fasce levabo, Ecl. 9, 65.

—stultitiam exuat, Pr. 35 ;

exuerint animum, Geo. 2, 51.

inlusa vestis, P. 14, 105 ;

inlusaque vestes, Geo. 2, 464.

Cf. also : C. 3, 76, and Ecl. 1, 80; Ps. 203, and Geo. 2, 302; S. 2, 800, and Aen. 1, 224 ; S. 2, 1024, Geo. 2, 223; P. 3, 8, and Aen. 11, 124 ; Ps. 27, and Aen. 7, 461; Ps. 707, and Aen. 2, 74.

For further imitation compare :

Prud.	Verg.	Prud.	Verg.
C. 3, 71	Geo. 2, 116	Ps. 112	Aen. 6, 156
C. 9, 90	Aen. 5, 277; Geo. 3, 421	Ps. 125	Aen. 5, 259
C. 9, 105	Aen. 5, 452	Ps. 435	Aen. 8, 696
C. 4, 58	Geo. 4, 132	Ps. 517	Geo. 3, 480
P. 10, 742	Aen. 1, 664	S. 1, 48	Aen. 8, 322
P. 10, 1015	Aen. 7, 612	S. 1, 559 and 560	Aen. 6, 235
C. 3, 101	Aen. 6, 638	S. 2, 340	Geo. 1, 62
C. 3, 186	Aen. 6, 730	S. 2, 408	Geo. 1, 375
A. 339	Geo. 2, 31	S. 2, 676	Aen. 10, 908
A. 612	Aen. 8, 687	S. 2, 967	Aen. 5, 744
S. 2, 335	Aen. 2, 10	Ps. 685	Aen. 8, 702
S. 2, 1032	Aen. 5, 273	Ps. 803	Aen. 9, 262
S. 2, 947	Geo. 2, 34	S. 2, 731	Aen. 4, 684
Ps. 51	Aen. 2, 277		

§151. **Imitation of Other Poets.** The poems of Prudentius show by their phraseology in particular that he had a wide

acqu tintance not only with the greater, but also with the lesser
poets of Rome, and that he deserves the title Gennadius bestowed
upon him, " vir saeculari litteratura eruditus."

a) *Horace.* Breidt' has shown what extensive use Prudentius
made of Horace. It appears that to the 238 passages he has
cited, every poem has contributed something except Cath. 12 ;
that the lyric poems have presented a third more than the hexa-
metric ; that the Peristeph. shows more passages imitated than the
Cath. (77 : 60) ;' that the odes are cited most often, then the epistles, then the satires. Some Horatian constructions also occur,
cf. §93, 108 d, et al.

b) *Ovid.* These may be cited : imbrem *flere facit.* C. 5, 24,
and me *flere facit,* Met. 7, 690; mollis si *bractea* gypsum
texerat, S. 1, 436; tenuis *bractea* ligna *tegat,* A. A. 3, 232.
Christum sub *tacito* pectore *murmurans,* Spr. 1, 36 ; —*tacito*
venerantur *murmure* numen, M. 6, 203. Cf. also, P. 2, 123,
and Fast. 2, 573 ; Ps. 573 and Ex. Pont. 3, 3, 9 ; C. 2, 69, and
Ex. Pont. 3, 3, 97 ; Ps. 414. and Met. 8, 530. To these parallels
in phraseology certain parallels in syntax may be added : emerere
with infin., according to Draeger §420, occurring only in Ovid, is
used by Prud. A. 1033; dedignor, frequent in Ovid, occurs in H.
955 ; piamen, a word used only by Ov., according to Harper's
Dict., occurs in C. 9, 33.

c) *Juvenal* seems to have been used more freely :
—*et frigida parvas*
praebebat spelunca domos, S. 2, 288 and Juv. 6, 34.
porrum et cepe, S. 2, 867, and Juv. 159 (Hor. Ep. 1, 2, 21).
genua incerare Dianae, A. 457 ;
genua incerare deorum, Juv. 10, 55.
Quidquid agunt homines, H. 763, and Juv. 1, 85.
—*in fornice natos,* H. 636 ; —*e fornice nati,* Juv. 3, 156.
—*vultuque et* voce *severa,* Ps. 553 ;
—*vultuque et* veste *severum,* Juv. 14, 110.
—*tenui distantia* fine, A. 748 ;
—*tenui distantia* rima, Juv. 3, 97.
—*ornamenta deorum,* S. 2, 64, and Juv. 3, 218.
For further imitations compare :

' Breidt, De Aurelio Prudentio Clemente Horatii Imitatore, 1887. A short
list is given by Faguet, De Aur. Prud. Clem. Carm. lyr. p. 54 (1883).

' Boissier, La Fin Pag. II, 117, however, says : " L'originalité du poète y
est à ce qu'il me semble, encore plus apparente que dans le recueil précé-
dent (Cath.) " Cf. also Ebert, Gesch. d. Lit. des Mitt. I', p. 281.

Prud.	Juvenal.	Prud.	Juvenal.
A. 485	1, 130	(H. 156	3, 30)
S. 2, 557	8, 3	Ps. 183	6, 502
S. 2, 866	15, 10	Ps. 555	14, 111
P. 2, 514	6, 343	S. 1, 257	6, 599
Praef. 24	9, 129	S. 2, 1094	10, 333
S. 1, 581	6, 349	S. 2, 1095	3, 158
H. 125	14, 136	S. 2, 1099	3, 36
S. 1, 338	1, 19	P. 10, 143	10, 35
H. 156	3, 30	P. 10, 700	11, 68
S. 2, 686	6, 190		

d) *Seneca.* The dependency of Prudentius upon Seneca and Lucan, not only for turns of expression, but also for models of whole scenes, has been pointed out by Sixt, Phil. 51 (1892), p. 501 f. Thus, the passage in P. 11, 85 f. seems to have been modeled on Sen. Phaedr. 1073 f.; C. 9, 70, on Herc. Fur. 46 f. For turns of expression Sixt points out 37 parallels, 17 being in the Cath. This subject has been further treated also by Weyman in Comment. Wölffl. (1891), p. 284. Cf. also Boissier, La Fin du Pag. 2, 122.

e) *Lucan.* With Lucan, Prudentius shares the same predilection for bloody scenes and details of horror (Sixt, p. 505): Bell. Civ. III, 572 f., and 6, 540 f., which seem to have served Prud. in his martyr-scenes. Cf. also Bell.·Civ. 9, 4 f., and Prud. P. 14, 91 f. On turns of expression cf. S. 2, 811 and Luc. 1, 110, C. 7, 163 and Luc. 4, 3, 14; Sixt cites 36 such passages, and of these 15 are in the Cath.

f) *Silius.* Pun. 6, 110 has the expression, sed quid ego haec = Prud. A. 741, but this may have come from Aen. 2, 101, and that from Ennius Ann. 210.

g) Two passages suggest *Statius :*
C. 3, 133: dumque rudes imitatur avos, rudes populos—colebas, Silv. 3, 3, 5; adflatum calido contraxit ab Euro, S. 2, 962. —Sic afflantur vineta noto, Silv. 5, 1, 146.
Note: Prudentius does not begin any of his verses with haud mora as does Vergil, but in A. 755 with nec mora as in Theb. 513 and Silv. 3, 117.

h) *Juvencus.* Only a few passages suggest this poet:
—*timor omnis abesto*, S. 2, 737, and Juv. 3, 107.
non ante *caeli* principem *septemplicis*, C. 7, 36 ;
—*caeli septemplicis* aethra, Juv. 1, 356.
—*per* utrumque *cucurrit*, A. 177 ;
per inane *cucurrit*, Juv. 1, 360.

Cf. also, P. 6, 160, and Praef. of Juv. 22; Prud. Ditt. 105, and
Juv. 1, 247; H. 330, and Juv. 1, 92, but also in Verg.; C. 5, 27,
and Juv. 2, 2, but cf. Stat. Theb. 2, 527; S. 1, 6, 85.

Note. No attempt has been made to trace in detail the phrases
imitated from the eccles. writers. Some of these imitations have
been already pointed out:
Brockhaus, Aur. Prud. Clem. p. 203 ff. calls attention to the
dependence of Prudentius on Tertullian; Ebert, Gesch. Litt. der
Mitt. I², 254 and 272, to his imitations of Ambrose; Manitius,
Gesch. d. Christ.-lat. p. 85 and 95, to his use of Damasus; and
p. 41, to his imitation of Commodian. Cf. also, Brand, De
Lactantii apud Prud. vestigiis (Heidl. 1894).

VII.—LANGUAGE.

§152. **Words used only by Prudentius.** Prudentius
exhibits a remarkable fondness for coining new words, or in
using old words in a new sense. Some of these were taken up
by later writers, but the following list of 55 is believed to contain
words used only by Prudentius. (Puech, it may be noted, on
p. 265, cites Krenkel's Diss. p. 3, for a list of such words, but here
only 6 are given.)

List (words marked * are ἅπ. εἰρ. only in sense used): bractealis,
P. 10, 1025; calcatrix, Ps. 587; caniformis, A. 195; *captator,
P. 5, 19; centifidus, S. 2, 890; Christipotens, S. 2, 710; cinisculus, C. 10, 143; circumsaltans, S. 1, 135; concrepito, P. 11, 56;
condomo, C. 7, 98; congregatim, C. 7, 143; conlaudabilis, H.
692; conperpetuus, A. 271 (Harper's Dict. and also Georges
cite it as A. 339); cunctiparens, P. 14, 128 (cunctipotens, P. 7, 56;
cf. mistakes in Harper's, §154); deliquium, H. 751; digestim,
P. 2, 129; digladiabilis, C. 3, 148; dissertator, A. 782; dolatus,
Ps. 835; excussus, P. 5, 226; exfibulo, Ps. 633; falsificatus, H.
549; flavicomans, A. 495; [fuliginosus, P. 10, 261 (?)]; incruente,
P. 10, 1094; inficiatrix, Ps. 630; innoto, C. 6, 128; inpressus, Ps.
273; (inspatior, A. 130, reading of Fabr. Gis. Weitz); lancinator,
P. 10, 1057; [lembulus, P. 5, 455(?)]; linteolus, P. 3, 180; [omni-
genus, S. 1, 13 (?)]; *praefulcio, P. 5, 335; *prosubigo, P. 3, 130;
pulvinarius, P. 10, 1056 (or gen. plur. of pulvinar?); *reglutino,
P. 10, 874; religamen, Ps. 359; ructamen, H. 466; russeolus, P.
11, 130; *salix (osier), P. 10, 703; saxigenus, C. 5, 8; scandalum,
Apr. 35; semetra, Ps. 829; speculamen, A. 20; spurcamen, C. 9,
56; strangulatrix, P. 10, 1103; subiugalis, P. 10, 333; subtacitus,

H. 174; tauricornis, P. 10, 222 ; Tibricola, P. 11, 174; tripictus,
A. 381 ; turbidulus, A. 208 ; tutaculum, S. 2, 388 ; ululamen, C.
10, 114 ; unicultor, P. 13, 90 ; urbicremus, H. 727 ; verberator,
P. 9, 38.

§153. **Titles.** Prudentius, like his fellow-countryman Juvencus, exhibits a fondness for introducing high-sounding titles for
divine personages, often accumulating epithet upon epithet, as in
A. 393, with its 12 epithets; (Manitius gives some examples in
Rhein. Mus. 45 (1890), 487).

a) *Titles of Christ:* salvator, P. 1, 115 ; C. 1, 50; parens
hominis, P. 13, 56 ; O splendor, O virtus Patris, factor orbis et
poli, atque auctor horum moenium, P. 2, 413 ; sermo Patris, C. 3,
141 ; sancte, C. 2, 69; optime, P. 7, 79 ; inventor rutili luminis, dux
bone, C. 5, 1 ; Nazarene, C. 7, 1, etc.; nostri mediator et omnipotens, A. 174 ; O crucifer bone, lucisator, verbigena, etc., with 5
lines in the address, C. 3, 1 ; paternae gloriae splendor, P. 10, 468 ;
cunctipotens, P. 7, 56; salutifer, P. 13, 91 ; Dominus, C. 3, 11 ; P.
3, 136 ; 7, 72. Also called Deus: C. 5, 127 ; P. 4, 9.

b) *Titles of God:* summe Pater, C. 5, 157 ; Pater supreme, C.
6, 1 ; caeli principem septemplicis, C. 7, 36; magister, Apr. (2) 1 ;
tonans, A. 171 ; H. 669; C. 6, 81 ; 12, 83 ; P. 6, 98 ; 10, 277 ; Ps.
640; H. 376; (also in Juv.) conditor, A. 807 ; conditor orbis, A.
894 ; Aeternus, A. 850 ; omnipotens genitor Christi et creator
orbis, P. 13, 55 ; Pater, C. 5, 25 ; Pater supreme, C. 6, 1 ; omnipa-
ter, P. 3, 70 ; omniparens, S. 2, 477, (omnigenus, S. 1, 13) ; omni-
pollens, Apr. 19 ; cunctiparens, animae dator, H. 931. Cf. also P.
14, 128 ; C. 2, 105 ; S. 1, 625 ; 2, 768; etc. Also called Christus :
C. 4, 68 ; D. 24.

§154. **Supplement to Harper's Latin Dictionary.** The
following list of words is designed to supplement the last edition
of Harper's Latin Dictionary (New York, 1880), but chiefly to
make some corrections in references made to Prudentius. It is
the conviction of the writer that all the references to Prudentius
need a careful revision. The following list is by no means complete; some the most conspicuous variations from the readings of
the editions of Arevalo, and of Dressel, are pointed out. No
attempt has been made to note the many occurrences of usages
both common and rare found in Prudentius, of which no mention
has been made in the Dictionary. Nor have divergences of one,
two, or three lines been noted.[1]

---

[1] Many of the references to certain lines in the Apotheosis may be found in
Dressel's edition by subtracting 68 from the number of the line cited.

abigo, to drive away : pax inde abigit bellum, Ps. 632.

accingo, in pass. (mid.?), to make one's self ready : accingere, nequissime, P. 10, 421.

accipitrina, marked *, but cf. Plaut. Bacch. 274.

advolitans, line not given ; see S. 2, 575.

aenipes, S. 1, 351, and not S. 1, 531.

aequiparabilis, marked : perh. only in Plaut., but cf. H. 79 : aequiparabile quidquam.

aetatula, a short period, P. 10, 614 ; cf. 677, used concretely.

alter-uter, H. 772 ; alterutram calcare viam.

anne in direct questions, Cic. only cited ; cf. S. 1, 400 : anne fides dubia est tibi ? also Claud. 26, 524 ; Ioh. Cass. 300, 14.

antiquitas, the history of ancient times, marked : only in prose, cf. P. 10, 32.

anulla, a little old woman, P. 6, 149 ; word not given (anicla, however, is cited for this passage ; but cf. Luc. Mueller, Re Metr.¹, p. 515).

Apenninicola, marked as ἅπ. εἰρ., but cf. S. 2, 521.

aroma, in sing., P. 14, 72, not 8 ; Plur. not noted ; cf. P. 10, 363.

argilla, white clay, H. 190 : viderat argillam simulacrum et structile.

aureolus, P. 3, 197, not 9, 196 ; also H. 272 ; S. 1, 640.

aurulentus, P. 12, 49 and not P. 6, 49.

azymon, A. 353 and not 421.

bracteola, Ps. 335 and not 355.

bubulcus, a herdsman (rare), cf. P. 10, 195 ; only Dig. cited.

bucula (Verg. only) cited ; cf. Pspr. 31.

caniformis, A. 195 and not 263.

cavillo (abl.), a rare word : P. 2, 318 ; not cited also by Georges, Wörtb.

cervicula, a small neck ; P. 10, 836.

chartula, a small book ; P. 1, 75 ; 10, 1115.

cinisculus, C. 10, 143, not 149.

circulus, P. 1, 72, not marked as a dimin. (cf. Archiv, 4, 187).

cluo, ere. In addition to authors cited, is used also by Plautus, Seneca, Ennodius, Cyprian Gall., Ven. Fortunatus. Cf. §2.

coinquino, to defile : monumenta coinquinet, S. 1, 505.

commemini, in Plautus, and rare ; P. 11, 231 : si bene commemini, colit hunc pulcerrima Roma.

conceptaculum, rare ; add Ps. 742 ; P. 10, 781.

confoveo, add Prud. 11, 138; Aug. C. Jul. 3, 15, 29, and Vulgate.

congregatim, marked *, but cf. also Aug. adv. quinque haer. 2, 3.

conluco, ēre, to be bright, P. 5, 10; omitted.

*conperpetuus, A. 271, not 339, as, also, in Georges, and Forcellini.

conventiculum (Juvenc. 2, 583), not a dimin., cf. Archiv, 4, 177.

corpusculum, a little body, an atom ; P. 10, 803; H. 595.

cujas, -atis, pron. interrog. Ps. 708; no author after Apuleius cited.

cuius, a, um, pron. rel. Praef. 33 ; rare.

cunctipotens marked *, but cf. also Ambrose, 81, 37 and 82, 25; and Aug. Spicul. 16.

deliramentum marked : in Plaut. and post Aug. prose; but cf. A. 200.

demutabilis, A. 276, not 344.

dicio marked: in plur. once ; but cf. Psych. 221; S. 2, 420. Also in sing.: H. 19, 408, etc.

diecula, only Plaut., Ter. and Apul. cited ; cf. C. 7, 96.

*digestim, P. 2, 129, not 3, 129.

dispendium, by-path: flexuosa corrigens dispendia, C. 7, 49; but means expense in Juv. 1, 46.

*dissertator, A. 783, not 850.

dissipator, marked *, but cf. Lucifer, of Cag., 133, 11.

dissociabilis, that cannot be united, Ps. 763.

dubitabilis, A. 581, not 649.

ecclesiastes, in sense of ecclesia, P. 10, 43: ire mandat milites ecclesiasten.

effrenis, e, add Prud. S. 1, 518 to list of occurrences.

eminulus, Varro only cited ; P. 3, 122: eminulis digitis.

executor, expounder, interpreter, P. 13, 16.

fasciola, add S. 2, 1008 to list of occurrences.

flammicomus, Ps. 775, is marked *, but Avien. also is cited.

floccus—the genitive of price, flocci is marked ante-class.; cf. P. 10, 140: flocci fecero.

fonticulus, only Hor. and Pliny cited ; cf. C. 5, 116.

ganea, not ganeum, in Ps. 343.

grunnitus, a rare word, only Cic. cited ; add P. 10, 993.

holusculum, add S. 2, 866, and P. 10, 262.

inculpabilis, A. 946, not 1015.

indelibilis, marked Ovidian, but occurs in P. 10, 1132.

induperator, S. 1, 147, marked archaic; but cf. Archiv, 1, 62.

impos, Prud. C. 9, 53; Ps. 585: mentis inpos.

impossibilis, see §119.

intemperans, incapable: tacendi intemperans, P. 2, 253.

interfundo, pour among, or through: animas hominum venis intus interfusas intelligo, Prud. S. 2, 380.

lacteolus, add Ps. 792; P. 3, 165; 11, 245.

lānienus, a is short, not long as given.

ligula, in sense of tongue, not cited; cf. P. 10, 978: quae concrepare ligula moderatrix facit.

luteolus, only Verg. and Col. cited; cf. Ps. 354.

malesanus (the reading of Arev. Obb. Dressel) occurs Ps. 203; H. 93; is not given by Harper's.

medela, a healing, only Gell. and Apul. cited; cf. C. 4, 85; 8, 77; 9, 36; 10, 83; A. 693. H. 663. S. 1, 6; 526. P. 1, 20; 2, 580; 6, 160; 9, 64; 10, 505. Also Juvenc. 1, 437; 2, 232; 356; 587. 3, 372.

medens, a physician; only Lucr. and Ov. cited for poet., add P. 10, 497.

mensurabilis, A. 813, not 881.

mixtim is marked *, but cf. P. 6, 141; 10, 848; H. 78; A. 1008; S. 2, 420.

natatus, us; add Prud. P. 10, 1054.

nemō, A. 173, 197; H. 85, 735; S. 1, 314; 2, pr. 56; 241; 471; 572; P. 1, 13; 10, 237.

nigellus, blackish; marked ante-class. Cf. P. 10, 156: lapis nigellus.

Nilicola, S. 2, 494, not 439. Used also by Gregory of Tours, h. F. 1, 10 (p. 39, 2).

numne, cited only for Plaut., Ter. and Cic., but occurs in S. 1, 322; 2, 940; H. 871.

oblectamen, marked: perh. only in plur., but cf. C. 7, 18; H. 311, 550; S. 2, 145; P. 2, 392.

obsequela, marked: ante-class. and in Sall.; but cf. C. 7, 51; 8, 19; P. 6, 78; Epil. 32.

offensaculum, Apr. 33, not A. 45; also Ps. 484, 781.

paeniteo, to repent, be sorry; S. 1, 517: ubi agros videt, paenitet.

palmula, an oar, P. 5, 462.

parabsis, a quadrilateral dish (Heins.), occurs in Ps. 532; Epil. 18.

paradiscola, H. 928, not 936.

piaclum, P. 10, 219, not P. 14; also piaculum, a sin, A. 544, P. 10, 1047.

piamen, marked *, occurs also in Ov. F. 3, 333; also in Prud. C. 9, 33.

praevenio, to outstrip, to prevent: sensum doloris mors cita praevenit, P. 14, 90; cf. also P. 10, 71.

profanator, A. 178, not 246.

promisce, only Cic., Liv., and Gell. cited; P. 10, 253.

propitio, -are, P. 3, 215, not 211.

propola, H. 761; no occurrence later than Cicero noted.

prostibulum, a prostitute, Ps. 92.

pudet used personally, only Plaut., Ter., and Luc. cited; cf. Prud. S. 1, 512, and P. 2, 177.

puellula, add C. 9, 110; P. 3, 103; 14, 11.

pugillus, C. 10, 144, not 152.

recrementum, Apr. 54, not 65.

remeabilis, A. 1049, not 1117.

reparatio, C. 10, 120, not 128.

resolubilis, used with caementum in A. 515, not 581.

rusticulas, adj. S. 1, 107: rusticulas lupas.

saeculum, P. 2, 583; not a dimin., cf. Archiv, 4, 177; seclum, C. 11, 79.

scalpellum, a scalpel; P. 10, 500; 902.

scandalum, lit. a stumbling-block; marked *; but cf. also Ps. 452; change 47 praef. Apoth. to 35 praef.

scintilla, a spark, A. 920. A dim.?

sentus, A. 55, not 123.

separ: separe ductu, A. 243, not 311.

sepulcralis, marked Ovidian, but cf. Ditt. 141, and S. 1, 97.

sigilla (orum), images, P. 10, 151; also in sing., an image (this usage not cited at all) P. 10, 233: sigillum adfixum Iovi avis ministrae.

sigillatus, H. 745, not 707.

signaculum, in sense of signum: a sign, A. 294; a standard, a banner, S. 1, 567.

sordeo, to seem base, impers.: si sordet venerarier et placet, H. 106.

sordidulus, low, base, marked *; but cf. S. 1, 69: sordidulam rapinam (Georges and Forcel. fail to cite this use).

spectamen, spectacle, marked Appul., but cf. Ps. 913.

speculamen, A. 20, not 88.

sphera, A. 210, not 278.

sprerunt (sperno), Ditt. 123, not 31.

stipis, gift, donation, S. 2, 911 ; for stips.

sufflabilis, A. 838, not 906.

supino, to turn backwards; supinat faciem, Ps. 281.

taeniola, only Col. cited; cf. S. 2, 1106. (Georges, and also Forcel., only cites Col.)

Tibricola, P. 11, 174, not 4, 174.

tradux, A. 915, not 983.

turbidulus, A. 208, not 276.

ungula, P. 1, 44; not marked as a dimin. (cf. Archiv, 4, 179).

ustuire occurs in P. 10, 885.

vago, -are, marked : ante-class., but cf. C. 6, 29.

vastatrix, marked *, but cf. also Sen., intpr. Iren. 1, 31, 4.

Vaticanus, adj. S. 1, 583.

veniabilis, H. 935, not 943.

virguncula, add also, S. 1, 64.

vitiabilis, A. 1045, not 1113.

volupe is marked ante-class., but cf. P. 9, 41, and MSS. reading of Arnobius, 268, 19 (Reiff), also Aug. Ep. 3, 5; Mart. Cap. 9, 888, Sidon. Ep. 22, 14.

zizania, Apr. 56, not A. 6, 8.

APPENDIX.

§155. **Recent Literature relating to Prudentius.**

G. Sixt: Die lyrischen Gedichte des Prudentius. Progr. Karls-gymnasium, Stuttgart, 1889.

M. Manitius: Beiträge zur Geschichte frühchristlicher Dichter im Mittelalter. Sitzungsber. d. phil. Akad. zu Wien, 1889, XII, p. 26.

M. Manitius: Zu Juvencus und Prudentius. Rhein. Mus. 45 (1890), p. 485.

G. Sixt: Zur neueren Litteratur über Prudentius. Korrespond-enz-Blatt. f. d. Gelehrten, Würtemberg, Mai u. Juni, 1891.

Carl Weyman: Seneca und Prudentius. Commentationes Woelfflinianae (1891), pp. 281–287.

M. Manitius: Geschichte d. Christlich-Lat. Poesie. Stuttgart, 1891.

G. Sixt: Des Prudentius Abhängigkeit von Seneca und Lucan. Phil. 51 (1892), pp. 501–506.

M. Manitius: Philologisches aus alten Bibliotheks-Katalogen. Rhein. Mus. 47 (1892), Suppl. pp. 95–101.

A. Zaniol: Aurelio Prudenzio Clemente, Poeta lirico-epico. Seconda edizione, Venice, 1890.

S. Brand: De Lactantii apud Prudentium vestigiis. Heidelberg, 1894.

Boissier: La Fin du Paganisme. Deux. ed. 1894, vol. II, pp. 105–152.

LIFE.

I was born April 8, 1863, at New Berlin, Pa., and received my preparatory training at Woodward High School, Cincinnati, Ohio. In 1885 I graduated from the Ohio Wesleyan University with the degree of A. B., and received the degree of A. M. in 1888. The following two years I taught Latin and German at the Little Rock University, and then taught for four years at the University of the Pacific as Adjunct Professor of Latin and Greek. In October, 1891, I entered Johns Hopkins University, where I pursued courses in Latin, Greek and Sanskrit under Professors Warren, Gildersleeve and Bloomfield, to each of whom I beg leave to express my sincere thanks, not only for the instruction given, but also for their many acts of kindness, which were to me both an encouragement and an inspiration.

> "His ego pro meritis quae praemia digna rependam,
> Non habeo."—[*Prud. Contr. Sym. II,* 750.

But to Professor Warren especially, as my chief adviser, I feel under many obligations both for his constant kindness and for his words of counsel so freely and generously given. In June, 1892, I was appointed Fellow in Latin; in October, 1893, Fellow by Courtesy, and on June 14, 1894, I received the degree of Ph. D.

www.ingramcontent.com/pod-product-compliance
Lightning Source LLC
Chambersburg PA
CBHW020040030726
47499CB00007B/2516